THE HONEYMOON ENDS

Caitlin looked for Jed's bright red wet suit among the other surfers. Standing up to get a better view, she saw him catch the swell of a wave. She watched the wave build and then begin to break in a long line of white foam. Jed was right on top of it. Nearby, someone said, "Hey, check out that guy in red! Good, isn't he?"

He is! she thought with pride. She wanted to turn and tell the person who'd spoken that the guy in red was her husband, but just then someone standing beside her gasped loudly. Jed was down, gone. Right in front of her eyes, he'd been sucked under by a giant wave.

"Jed, no!" she screamed wildly. Tears sprang to her eyes.

"What happened?" a man asked. "Where's the guy in red?"

"He wiped out," his friend answered.

"I know, but where is he?"

"I don't know. I can't see him. I'm going to get the paramedics. He's going to need 'em when he comes up."

"If he does. That wave was a killer."

Killer . . . The word ran over and over in Caitlin's mind as she desperately searched the blue-green water for a sign of her husband. . . .

Bantam Books in the Caitlin series
Ask your bookseller for the books you have missed

TOGETHER FOREVER

Created by
Francine Pascal

Written by
Diana Gregory

BANTAM BOOKS
TORONTO · NEW YORK · LONDON · SYDNEY · AUCKLAND

TOGETHER FOREVER
A BANTAM BOOK 0 553 26863 5

First publication in Great Britain

PRINTING HISTORY
Bantam edition published 1988

Bantam Books are published by Transworld Publishers
Ltd., 61–63 Uxbridge Road, Ealing, London W5 5SA, in
Australia by Transworld Publishers (Australia) Pty. Ltd.,
15–23 Helles Avenue, Moorebank, NSW 2170, and in New
Zealand by Transworld Publishers (N.Z.) Ltd., Cnr. Moselle
and Waipareira Avenues, Henderson, Auckland.

Printed and bound in Great Britain by
Cox & Wyman Ltd., Reading, Berks.

TOGETHER
FOREVER

1

"There's absolutely no question about it," Melanie Michaels said, bubbling with excitement. As she nodded her head, the short light brown curls that framed her face swung softly. "You're going to be the most beautiful bride ever."

"Really? Do you really think Jed will like my dress?" Caitlin Ryan asked, her deep blue eyes full of concern. She was standing in the middle of her bedroom at Ryan Acres, while a dressmaker put the final touches on her wedding dress.

"Like it?" Melanie cried, her eyes opening wide. "Are you kidding?" Sitting cross-legged on one of Caitlin's twin canopied beds, she watched as the dressmaker basted another piece of lace into place on the satin bodice. "My brother is going to be so blown away when he sees you that he may faint."

Caitlin laughed delightedly. "Well, I'm not sure that's exactly how I want him to react when he sees me walking up the aisle." She looked into the mirror. Tipping her head slightly, she studied her reflection. "You don't think the neckline is—well, a bit low? The shoulders, I mean. Maybe we should add some more lace there, too."

"It looks great," Melanie said with a grin. "You were absolutely right about the front, though—it does look better with the lace panel. But you've got great shoulders, and you should show them off. Besides, you've still got a fabulous tan."

"I'm glad about that," Caitlin replied. "I'd really hate to show up on the beach in Waikiki on our honeymoon looking pale."

"Hawaii's going to be so beautiful. And your hotel looked absolutely luxurious in the brochure you showed me," Melanie said. Then, involuntarily, she let out a little sigh. "Oh, I'm so jealous, Caitlin. I wish Howard and I were getting married."

"Don't rush it," Caitlin said, advising her with a warm smile. "You've got plenty of time. If you think about it, it was only a couple of months ago that you thought you absolutely hated him."

2

She thought back to earlier that summer, and she found it difficult to believe that Melanie and Howard had ever hated each other. But they had. Howard Josso was the attorney who had helped Caitlin protect Ryan Mining from her old enemy, Colin Wollman, that past summer. Caitlin had inherited the company upon her grandmother's death in June, and without Howard's help and advice, she was sure she'd have lost Ryan Mining.

"It's funny, Melanie. You thought you were so crazy about that wimp Laurence Baxter all summer. But whenever you saw Howard, you'd get a sparkle in your eyes. And as soon as you left, he'd always ask me a million questions about you." Caitlin giggled. "Always very serious, of course."

Melanie laughed, too. "I was just stupid not to recognize what a jerk Laurence had become," she said. She waved her hand, dismissing any thought of Laurence. "Now I know what real love is, and I just want to make sure it lasts forever. The way your love for Jed will last."

"Mmmm. I know what you mean."

"Oh, I wish *I* was going to Hawaii, too," Melanie said lightly. Unfolding her legs, she slipped off the bed and walked over to the chaise, where Caitlin piled up the clothes she had bought for her wedding trip. Picking up a skimpy designer bathing suit, Melanie held it up in front of her, trying to imagine what it would look like on her. "I really love this suit. And all of your dresses are just gorgeous."

"I must admit, I had fun shopping for them," Caitlin said with a nod.

"Wow!" Dropping the bathing suit, Melanie picked up a camisole of the palest yellow silk, which was edged with lace. "Has Jed seen this? It's fabulous."

"He hasn't seen any of my trousseau. I want to surprise him." Caitlin's eyes twinkled.

"Well, you definitely will if you wear this," Melanie said, clearing her throat and winking. After carefully refolding the sheer camisole and putting it back into its tissue-lined box, she turned toward Caitlin and jokingly demanded, "You are going to remember to throw the bouquet in my direction, aren't you?"

"Don't you think that would be a little unfair?" Caitlin asked with a laugh.

"A little," Melanie said, agreeing and smiling. "But I figure if Howard sees me catch it, he may get the message." She walked back over to the bed and flopped down on it again. Glancing happily at the dress of pale amethyst silk, which hung on a padded hanger on one of the closet

4

doors, she hugged herself. "Besides, if I'm wearing that dress, how can he possibly resist me? I'm glad you let me get purple instead of the green the other girls are wearing. Howard won't stand a chance."

"He sure won't. That color really does look terrific on you."

"Speaking of the bridesmaids, have you heard from them all? Have they had their dresses fitted?"

"Ages ago," Caitlin said with an answering nod. "Carol and Jackie, sorority sisters from Carleton Hill, are driving up together from Richmond on Thursday night. And Diana Chasen will be flying in from California on Friday." Looking at Melanie, she said "Oh, that's right, you've never met her. She went to Highgate with me, and now she lives in Los Angeles."

"What about Morgan and Gloria?" Melanie asked. She knew Morgan Conway and Gloria Parks, who also had attended Highgate Academy, from New York. Caitlin's two high school friends had helped her find her way around New York after she graduated from Carleton Hill and got a job at *National News* as an editorial assistant. "Isn't there a problem with Gloria getting time off from work, or something?"

"Poor Gloria," Caitlin said sympathetically as

she raised her arm so the dressmaker could thread a pale pink satin ribbon through the lace on the sleeve. "Everything's all right now, though. Gloria called last week to say her boss did agree to let her have Friday off. I guess I forgot to mention it to you. Anyway, she and Morgan are flying down on Friday morning. Rollins is going to meet them, as well as Diana, at Dulles." Rollins, who had been with the Ryan family since Caitlin was a little girl, served as both chauffeur and butler. "They should get here in plenty of time for the bridesmaids' luncheon."

"Mmmm, I saw the menu. Mrs. Crowley was tacking it up on the bulletin board in the kitchen this morning when I was having my coffee. Sounds delicious."

"I'm glad you think so," Caitlin said honestly. "I thought shrimp salad would be special, but light. I didn't want anything too heavy before the rehearsal, and then there's the rehearsal dinner later."

Melanie nodded.

"I was also thinking it might be nice to have lunch out on the terrace, if it's sunny."

"That's a terrific idea," Melanie said. "The weather is supposed to hold."

"Hmmm. And if it's as warm as it is today, we can swim." The dressmaker was ready to work

6

on the other sleeve then, and Caitlin turned to accommodate her. "Oh, speaking of the pool, Emily suggested that I ask the florist to make interlocking circles of gardenias to float on the pool," Caitlin said softly. "You know, as symbols of our wedding rings. It's probably too late, but I thought I'd ask."

The Emily they were talking about was Emily Michaels Kent, Jed and Melanie's cousin. She was another bridesmaid, as well as a close friend of Caitlin's from Highgate. Emily had been the first of Caitlin's friends to be married, and she and her husband, Jim, lived in a huge old farmhouse not far from Ryan Acres.

"Oh, how romantic!" Melanie said. "I love it."

"And especially since we're having the reception outside on the—"

"Oh, no!" Melanie slapped her forehead. "I forgot to tell you. The caterer called a little while ago, when you were out shopping. I'm supposed to tell you that they're having some problems getting the pink and white striped tent, and they want to know if yellow and white would be okay."

"Oh, darn!" A tiny frown marred Caitlin's smooth forehead. "I really did want—Oh, well, I'll call them back this afternoon." She shrugged philosophically. "The wedding plans have gone so smoothly. If the color of the tent is the only problem, I think I can live with it."

"They said they would call back, and that—" Melanie stopped in midsentence as the phone on the bedside table rang. "I'll get it."

"Thanks," Caitlin said.

"Hello," Melanie answered. She smiled, then put her hand over the mouthpiece. "It's for me," she said happily. "Howard."

Caitlin raised her eyebrows, then grinned back. While the dressmaker continued her work, adding pink ribbon to the hem, Caitlin turned to look out the window. Lost in thought, she stared at the deep blue late-summer sky and the rolling green pastures, separated from the formal front lawn and curving drive by white-painted fences. Sleek Thoroughbred horses grazed lazily on the lush grass.

Yes, she thought with a quiet happiness, so far her wedding plans had gone remarkably well. She felt lucky, especially considering the terrible events of the past summer—her grandmother's sudden death, her fight to keep Ryan Mining, Colin Wollman's scheming, and the loss of the lovely old Ryan Acres stables to fire. In a way, though, all those trials had almost been a blessing. They had made Caitlin and Jed realize that

8

they really belonged in Virginia at Ryan Acres and not in New York City.

And so Jed gave up his position at a prestigious law firm and moved down to Ryan Acres. He and Caitlin had decided to turn their mutual love of fine horses into a business—they would raise Thoroughbreds. Jed had grown up on a ranch in Montana, and he had spent a year at Montana Agricultural College, so he felt confident to manage a horse farm. And with Caitlin's knowledge of horses, they were sure to be a success.

Fortunately, there were so many bedrooms at Ryan Acres that there was space for Jed to stay there until the wedding. Once they were married, he and Caitlin would move into a new suite on the second floor. There was a master bedroom, done in shades of coral and beige, as well as two separate dressing rooms, a small sitting room, and two bathrooms. But the best part, at least to Caitlin, was the bay window and window seat she had had put in the bedroom. It brightened up the whole room.

Melanie, too, lived permanently at Ryan Acres. She had her own bedroom and private bath at the other end of the floor.

Caitlin knew she had never been happier— except for one thing. Her old friend, Ginny

Brookes, wasn't going to be a bridesmaid. In fact, she wasn't coming to the wedding. She had given a thin excuse. But Caitlin knew she wouldn't come without her boyfriend, Julian Stokes, who wasn't exactly welcome at Ryan Acres.

When Ginny first started seeing Julian, Caitlin had disapproved. She didn't believe for a minute that someone as evil as Julian had been could ever change. But he had convinced Ginny that he had. And Ginny couldn't forgive Caitlin for not believing him, too.

Caitlin thought of Julian and pictured his dark, handsome features and steely gray eyes. She remembered the year at Carleton Hill when she and Julian had been friends. She was going through a rough time with Jed, who was attending college in Montana for that year. Julian had moved in quickly, turning her against Jed and making her believe she was in love with him. It was all part of a scheme he had come up with to make Caitlin pay for all the advantages she had always enjoyed. The son of a miner, he had lived in a dirt-poor West Virginia town. Julian wanted the beautiful, rich Caitlin to share some of the shame and embarrassment he had felt most of his life.

Fortunately, she had discovered his terrible

plot before she and Jed were separated forever. But now Ginny was in love with Julian, and she insisted that he had changed. Could anyone change that much? Caitlin wondered.

Oh, well, she thought, letting out a little sigh. She couldn't protect Ginny from getting hurt. The girl was too stubborn. She'd never believe that Julian was no good unless she, too, felt his cruelty.

"There you are, Miss Ryan." The seamstress's voice broke into Caitlin's thoughts, and she tore her gaze away from the scene outside the window. "I believe that's the last of it." The thin, gray-haired woman stood a few feet from Caitlin, beaming with satisfaction. "Would you like to see the complete picture? You could try on the veil, and see how it all looks."

"Oh, Caitlin, yes," Melanie said, jumping up from the bed. Finishing her conversation with Howard, she hung up the phone. She crossed the room to help the seamstress lift the pearl-studded crown that was attached to yards of tulle and fine Belgian lace from a shiny white box.

For the wedding, Caitlin's shoulder-length dark hair would be pulled up into a mass of ringlets, which would anchor the crown. Now, Melanie and the older woman just set the beaded circlet gently onto her head. Then Melanie stood back as the dressmaker arranged the yards of fragile veil around Caitlin's head like a white cloud.

"Oooh," Melanie squealed. "You're gorgeous!"

"That you are, Miss Ryan. Why, in all my days as a dressmaker, I've never seen such a lovely bride."

"Well, it's all because of you. Thank you so much for coming over today. I was afraid it would be too late to make any changes, but the pink ribbons really look—"

A sharp knock on the door interrupted her. Caitlin froze.

There was another knock. "Hey, Caitlin," came Jed's slight western drawl. "It's getting late. Are you almost ready?"

"Late?" Melanie whispered, looking at Caitlin. "Late for what?"

"Are you dressed?" Jed called. "Can I come in?"

"*No!*" Melanie shrieked. "Don't you dare!" Rushing across the room, she leaned against the door to stop Jed from coming in. "Caitlin has her wedding dress on, and it's bad luck for the groom to see the bride in her dress before the ceremony."

"Okay, okay," Jed answered, laughing. "I won't come in. Are you going to be much longer, Caitlin? We really should be leaving pretty soon."

"Oh, my gosh!" Caitlin's hand flew over her mouth as she glanced at the gold clock on the mantle above the fireplace. "Jed's right. I said I'd be ready to go right this minute." She called out, "Give me a few minutes to change, Jed. I'll meet you downstairs in ten minutes, okay?"

"Meet me out front," Jed called back. "I'll go get the car and bring it around. That is, if you really will be ready in ten minutes." He chuckled. "Usually when you say ten, it's more like twenty."

"And you're already acting like a husband," Caitlin said lightly. "Now go on. Go get the car. By the time you pull up to the front steps, I'll be there waiting for you."

"We'll see about that," Jed said doubtfully. Then they heard his footsteps moving away, down the hall.

"Quick," Caitlin said with a smile. "Help me out of this." She reached up to take off the crown and veil. "I want to prove to him that I really can be ready in ten minutes."

"Where are you two going?" Melanie asked, starting to unbutton the back of Caitlin's dress as the seamstress put the veil back in its box. "Someplace special?"

"We're driving up to the Maryland breeders' sale," Caitlin replied, slipping her arms out of the sleeves. "Jed was looking through the catalog the other night and said he decided it might be a good idea to start checking out the major horse auctions. You know, to see what kind of prices different horses are going for these days."

"Well, I guess if you're going to breed horses for a living, it's the thing to do," Melanie said as she helped Caitlin out of the full-skirted dress. "But why this close to your wedding? You have so many other things to do."

"Actually, I think that might be exactly why Jed's so anxious to go to this sale," Caitlin replied. With a quick shake of her head, she went into her dressing room and flipped on the light. She opened the door to the walk-in closet.

"You mean because a guy's supposed to get scared when it's so close to his wedding day?" Melanie shook her head. "Jed would never get cold feet, you know that. He loves you too much."

"Not cold feet exactly. I think maybe he's just a little nervous." Reaching in among the rows of clothes, she pulled out a pair of pleated cotton slacks. "Which is completely understandable,"

14

she said as she slipped a blue cotton sweater over her head. "To be honest, I'm a little nervous about the wedding myself. Sometimes I think that I have absolutely no right to be so happy, that something terrible has got to happen to ruin everything."

"Nonsense!" Melanie exclaimed. "You have every right to be happy, Caitlin. You're one of the best people I know."

"Oh, Melanie." Caitlin gave Jed's sister a quick hug. "You're right. It's so silly to worry."

"It sure is." Melanie suddenly grinned, and they both burst out laughing.

The dressmaker, although she hadn't heard what they had been saying, glanced over at the two girls and smiled. "I'll be leaving now, Miss Ryan. Your dress will be finished and ready for you on Wednesday."

"Thank you so much," Caitlin said. She nodded goodbye as the woman left.

Caitlin slipped her feet into a pair of comfortable leather flats. "You know, I'm really looking forward to an afternoon of concentrating on horses." Opening her jewelry box, she took out her favorite pearl earrings. "There," she said as she turned to Melanie for inspection. "How do I look?"

"Great!" Melanie answered, crossing her arms

and cocking her head, studying her friend. She glanced over at the little clock above the fireplace. "And in less than eight minutes, too. Be sure to tell Jed that," she added, grinning.

"Absolutely," Caitlin replied, picking up her purse.

"And have fun," Melanie called as Caitlin went to the door.

"I will. Promise." Caitlin turned the knob, then looked back. "Jed *and* a horse sale—how can I miss?" With a smile and a little wave she shut the door behind her.

2

A few minutes later Caitlin dashed through the front door and down the broad steps to where Jed was waiting for her in his new car.

She paused for a moment to admire the shiny blue BMW, then opened the door and slid inside. Settling against the plush softness of expensive tan leather, she asked sweetly, "Am I late?"

"Okay, okay." He grinned back, his mouth turned up in the crooked smile that Caitlin loved. "You won, but only because I teased you."

He ducked as Caitlin aimed a playful punch at him. Catching her hand, he pulled her toward him and kissed her softly.

As they parted, Caitlin leaned back in her seat

and looked over at Jed's rugged handsome face. A wave of love washed over her, and she reached up to run her hand through his wavy, light brown hair. "What a nice way to start the afternoon."

"I think so, too." Jed took Caitlin's hand and gave it a tender squeeze. "I'd kiss you again, but I think we'd better be on our way. I really want to get there before the sale begins."

With an understanding nod, Caitlin reached for her seat belt and buckled it. Jed put the car in gear and started down the long private drive, which was bordered by ancient oaks.

An hour later they had crossed into Maryland and were heading into serious horse country. Before long, Jed pulled the car into a large parking area, which surrounded a cluster of white barns. The lot was already jammed with other expensive cars, as well as many four-wheel-drive vehicles and horse trailers.

As they got out of the car, Caitlin could hear the horses nickering and she could smell the sweet hay and sawdust bedding. Taking a deep breath, she sighed happily. Horses were a definite passion in her life. Her heart beat a little faster as she walked around the car to join Jed.

Jed was holding the sales catalog, which had been sent to Ryan Acres a few weeks earlier.

"Shall we go straight to the barn?" he asked, taking her hand. "The bidding won't start for twenty minutes."

"Oh, let's," Caitlin said, agreeing. "We should get a closer look at some of the horses we read about."

"Then what are we waiting for?" Jed smiled, but Caitlin didn't notice. She was already walking across the graveled drive toward one of the long, low buildings.

They entered the first barn. Inside, it was spacious and cool, brightened occasionally by the sunlight that filtered in from the skylights overhead. People—potential buyers and casual onlookers, as well as sellers—were strolling down the corridor and stopping at times to study various horses. They were mostly yearlings, but a few two-year-olds and brood mares were up for auction, too.

Caitlin stopped at one stall to look at a lovely chestnut filly with an especially fine head. As Caitlin clucked softly at the horse, she turned to look at him. "What a sweetheart," Caitlin said admiringly. "Oh, Jed, wouldn't she look nice under saddle? I can just imagine her at the Appleveil Hunt in a couple of years."

"She is pretty. But how about this guy over here?" He deftly steered Caitlin across the aisle.

Looking into the stall, she saw a tall, handsome dappled gray. "Well, what do you think?" he asked, grinning.

"What would anyone think?" Caitlin replied. "He's probably the best horse here. His sire's Sleight of Hand," she said, naming one of the biggest money winners in horse racing. "Magic Man is a good name for him, too. He's going to be a winner."

"Yeah, I know." The grin on Jed's face was growing.

"He's gorgeous, Jed, but hardly hunter or jumper material. I mean, he's meant for racing. You don't waste breeding like this on hunting."

"I wasn't thinking of making him a hunter," Jed said almost casually.

"He is beautiful, though, isn't he?" Caitlin held out her hand, clucking to the finely muscled yearling. Suddenly Jed's words hit her. She turned toward him. "What did you say?"

He chuckled at the confused look on her lovely face. "I said, I'm not thinking of hunting him." He paused before saying, "I thought we might race him."

"Race him?" Caitlin's deep blue eyes widened. "Oh, Jed, are you really serious?" She looked at the colt and then back at Jed. "Are you honestly thinking of buying him?"

"For you," Jed said as he slipped an arm around her waist. "It's my wedding present to you."

"Oh, Jed!" Her eyes were glowing with happiness. "You're too good to be true," she cried, throwing her arms around his neck.

"I'm glad you think so," Jed replied. His green eyes were dancing. "I saw the listing for Magic Man in the catalog when it came to the house a couple of weeks ago, and I did a little checking on him. He could start his early training almost immediately, and maybe even be ready for his first race by spring."

"Imagine—a horse, racing in Ryan Acres colors." She laughed delightedly. "Wait, we don't even have colors."

"We do now," Jed said eagerly. "That's the other part of my surprise. I already registered the colors—rose and blue, if they're okay. There's even a set of silks hanging in the stable office back at Ryan Acres. The shirt and cap are light blue with the initials *RA* in rose. There's a single pink rose that runs across the initials."

"Jed, I don't know what to say." Caitlin's blue eyes glistened with tears of happiness.

"Just say you think it's a good idea," Jed replied, gently squeezing her waist.

"I'm so excited I could cry." Quickly rising

on her toes, she kissed him. "Jed Michaels, you are absolutely the most wonderful man in the world. I'm so lucky to be marrying you."

Looking as if he were curious about what was going on just outside his stall door, the gray colt poked his head out. Tentatively, he nuzzled Caitlin's arm.

With a slight start, she turned to look at him, then smiled. "And as for you, Magic, you're going to make it all perfect."

"But first we have to buy him," Jed reminded her, looking at his watch. "Think you can tear yourself away from him long enough to go—"

"I wouldn't if I were you," a low, gravelly voice said, warning them.

Caitlin turned to see a man walking directly up to them. He looked very serious.

"Excuse me, what did you say?" Jed's eyes narrowed slightly, and Caitlin could tell he was as suspicious of the man as she was.

The man was standing directly in front of them by then; he was barring them from going into the hallway that led to the sales barn. *That's strange*, Caitlin thought. *He doesn't look all that threatening.* He was very short, and well past middle age. His tan face was creased with wrinkles, and on his head he wore a flat tweed cap. A fringe of gray hair poked out from beneath the hat. Caitlin was almost certain he was a retired jockey.

"You look like a nice young couple," he said, obviously trying to sound more pleasant. "I couldn't help overhearing you talking about buying this here colt, and I thought you should know you're wasting your time bidding on him. Why don't you just pick another horse?" He nodded toward the rows of stalls on either side. "There're plenty to choose from."

"We aren't interested in other horses," Jed said evenly. "We are bidding on this one."

"But, you see, he's already spoken for." The man smiled. It was not a friendly smile.

"What do you mean, he's already spoken for?" Jed dropped his arm from around Caitlin's waist and stepped slightly in front of her. "I'm afraid that's not possible. This is an open sale—there are no presales."

"Not officially, no," the man said and glanced down at his feet for a moment. Then he looked back up. "But the horse is as good as sold, if you get my drift. . . ." The man's tone left little doubt as to what he meant. Someone had made a very private—and very illegal—deal with the auctioneer to buy Magic Man.

"Who do you work for?" Jed asked bluntly.

"It doesn't matter. Just take my advice; stay

away from that colt." The man touched the brim of his cap in a gesture of exaggerated politeness.

"You can forget your advice—" Jed started to say. But the man had already turned and was making his way down the still-crowded aisle toward the sales barn. Other people were beginning to move in that direction as well.

"Come on, Caitlin," Jed said, grimly taking her hand. "I want to make sure we have good seats. I want to be sure the auctioneer sees my bids."

After getting a bidding number, Caitlin and Jed found seats in the second row, almost directly in front of the auctioneer's podium. Several other yearlings were brought into the sales ring and sold before Magic Man. This was normal—the cheaper horses were always offered for sale first, in order to warm up the buyers.

Then finally the animated silver gray colt was led into the ring, and Caitlin and Jed overheard a whispered voice behind them. A man said to the person beside him, "That's the yearling Avil Horton has his eye on. Don't even bother reaching for your checkbook."

"You're right about that, Harry," the other man answered. "Avil Horton gets what he wants, no matter what. I sure wouldn't want to tangle with him."

*So that's who we're going to be bidding against—
Avil Horton*, Jed mused. He leaned over to
Caitlin, whispering directly in her ear. "Do you
know who this Horton guy is?"

Caitlin nodded. Whispering back, she said,
"He's big in horse circles in Virginia. I've ridden
in a few hunts where he was a guest." She
wrinkled her nose in distaste. "And I don't think
much of his manners. I've seen him practically
ride over a person to get over a fence first." She
shook her head. "I didn't know he was into
racehorses, though."

Jed nodded. "Well, if he is, he's not going to
get what he wants this time."

The auctioneer read off the catalog number for
Magic Man and then added that he was a prime
example of the progeny of the great Kentucky
Derby horse, Sleight of Hand. "Here, ladies and
gentlemen, is a future Triple Crown winner if
there ever was one." He looked around, checking the audience's reaction. "There is a reserve
on this horse, which means that I must start the
bidding at no less than five hundred thousand
dollars. Do I hear five—"

"Five hundred thousand." The bid came from
across the room.

Caitlin and Jed glanced at the man who had
made the bid. He was a balding man of medium

build, wearing a slightly rumpled tan suit. Beside him stood the short man they had just met in the barn.

"Five hundred twenty-five thousand," Jed called.

The man must be Avil Horton's manager, Caitlin guessed. And the short man could be the trainer.

"Do I hear five hundred fifty thousand?" the auctioneer called. The bald man nodded.

"Do I hear six hundred thousand?"

That time Jed held up his number and nodded.

"Seven hundred thousand?" Horton's man nodded.

The bidding seesawed between Jed and Horton's manager, going up in increments of fifty thousand dollars. No one else was even in the auction. Finally, after Jed nodded his bid of nine hundred thousand, the bidding slowed.

"Do I hear a million, sir?" The auctioneer was pointing his gavel toward the bald man. "Nine hundred fifty thousand?" he said, prompting him.

The short man said something to the manager, who then nodded. He held up his card.

"You, sir?" The auctioneer looked directly at Jed.

"Nine hundred and seventy-five thousand," Jed answered without hesitation.

As if they were watching a tennis match, everyone looked from Jed to Horton's man and back again. Now they all waited for the man to bid. In the near silence, Caitlin heard the quiet *whir* of the air conditioner. Someone coughed.

"Sir? I must have a bid, sir."

The man squared his shoulders. "One million dollars."

Several people gasped.

"One million. The bidding now stands at one million." The auctioneer turned to Jed. "Do I hear an answering bid?"

Everyone was now looking at Jed, including Caitlin, who was holding her breath.

Jed gave her a calm look, then turned to the auctioneer and nodded. "One million, one hundred thousand dollars."

Everyone in the room turned immediately and looked at Horton's man, who appeared worried. The short man spoke to him, and after a moment he shook his head. Looking at the auctioneer, he shook his head again.

His eyes wide with surprise, the auctioneer nodded his understanding. Glancing around the room, he asked the customary, "Anyone else?"

No one said a word.

"Anyone?" he repeated, glancing around the room once more. "Sold!" he cried, banging the gavel on the podium. "Catalog number one hundred thirty-nine, to the gentleman in the center of the second row for one million, one hundred thousand dollars."

Caitlin jumped up and gave Jed a quick, excited hug. Then they began to make their way along the line of seats toward the aisle. Magic Man had already been led away and another yearling was being led in. "We now have catalog number one hundred forty," Caitlin heard the auctioneer announce as Jed took her hand and led her toward the back of the room where the cashier's office was located.

Their business in the small, crowded office didn't take long. Jed had arranged for a line of credit beforehand, so there were no bank references to check. There were just some papers to be signed, and after that a time was set for Magic Man to be delivered to Ryan Acres.

"I still can't believe this is happening," Caitlin said as they left the building. They walked through the breezeway between the main building and the barn. "One million dollars! I never thought I'd own a horse that was worth that much."

"One point one million," Jed said, reminding

her, his mouth curving up in a teasing smile. "But then, who's counting?" Stopping, he turned and slipped his arms around her, drawing her close. "I love you, Caitlin," he said softly, then bent his head and kissed her.

A minute later, his arms still around her, he threw his head back and laughed. "Boy, did you see the look on Horton's manager's face? He was mad."

Caitlin nodded and agreed with a grin. "Did you get the feeling he'd been instructed to stop at a million?"

"Uh-huh. Well, so much for the little guy's threats. They lost and we won."

At Jed's words, Caitlin's face clouded over. "You don't suppose that Horton could really do anything to us, do you?"

"Absolutely not." Jed reassured her. "We own Magic fair and square now. What's he going to do, steal him?"

"I guess you're right," Caitlin said. Then, her voice bubbling with renewed excitement, she said, "Hey, he must be back in his stall by now. Can we go see him? I want to tell him he's ours."

Jed nodded and, arm in arm, they walked down the aisle to Magic Man's stall. The gray's head was sticking out of the open upper half of the stall, almost as if he were expecting them.

But just as Caitlin was about to reach out and stroke the horse's velvety nose, the man who had been bidding against them came around the corner. He obviously had something on his mind, and Jed and Caitlin were forced to stop where they were. Up close, Caitlin could see the man had small eyes of pale blue. There was a film of perspiration on his bald head. He looked mean.

Jed took a breath, about to say something, but the bald man beat him to it. "Enjoy your horse while you can, Mr. Michaels," he said. "Because he won't be yours for long. You made a very big mistake at that auction, very big. No one—and I mean no one—crosses Avil Horton and gets away with it."

"Now look here—" Jed began to reach out to the other man.

But just then a security guard stepped into view at the far end of the aisle and looked at both of them. Jed let his arms drop back to his sides.

The man nodded slightly to Jed, flashed him a warning smile, then walked away. "Good day," he said to the guard as he passed him.

"Oh, Jed!" Caitlin cried, taking his arm. "We'd better be careful. He looked awfully serious."

3

"Magic Man! Oh, I just love that name," Melanie cried when Caitlin told her about the colt. "It makes him sound so fast and powerful."

"He sounds like a real knockout." Howard took a sip of his white wine and smiled. "And you said he'll be arriving tomorrow?"

"Yes," Caitlin replied, looking across the table at Howard's handsome face. With his sandy-blond hair and piercing blue eyes, he looked a little like a young Robert Redford. "I'm so excited I don't think I'll be able to sleep at all tonight," she said, continuing. She smiled lovingly at Jed, who sat beside her. "Can you imagine a more wonderful wedding present?"

The four of them were having a leisurely dinner in the formal dining room at Ryan Acres.

Rollins had just cleared away the first course and was setting plates of grilled swordfish in front of them.

It had been several hours since the horrid encounter with Avil Horton's manager at the sale, and while Caitlin still felt a bit uneasy, she wasn't quite so frightened anymore. On the way home, Jed had done much to calm her fears by reminding her that there wasn't anything Horton could do to get Magic Man now. The manager was probably just afraid to tell Horton that he had lost the horse, Jed had reasoned. So he tried to bully them into giving up Magic Man.

"We've decided to begin training him right away," Jed was saying to the others. "I called Lou Becker after we got home this afternoon, and he's agreed to come over tomorrow to look at him."

"Lou Becker!" Melanie exclaimed. "Didn't he train last year's Derby winner?"

Caitlin nodded. "I think we'll be very lucky if we can get him to work with Magic. He only agrees to train horses that he thinks will go to the top."

"Actually, he already knows something about Magic," Jed said. "He suggested—whether or not he takes on his training—that we nominate him for the Dogwood Cup next July."

"Nominate him?" Howard asked, looking confused. "What exactly does that mean?" He wasn't so experienced with horses as the others—although he was learning. Melanie had been insisting that he go riding with her a few times a week, so he'd be ready to join the hunt when the fall season arrived.

"It's sort of like paying an entry fee," Caitlin explained. "If you think your horse has the potential to be ready for a particular race, especially a big one like the Dogwood Cup, you can assure him a place by paying a small, beginning fee."

"There are more fees as you get closer to the race," Jed said. "If your horse isn't progressing very well, you can drop out at anytime. For the owner, it minimizes the risk of losing a big chunk of money if his horse doesn't turn out as well as he thought. And, because lots of horses are nominated, it means a larger purse for the winners."

"That sounds reasonable," Howard said. He picked up a roll and buttered it. "So, are you going to do as this Lou Becker suggests and nominate Magic?"

"Umm-hmm." Caitlin put her hand over Jed's. "We discussed it before dinner. That's exactly what we're going to do."

Coming back into the room a moment later, Rollins cleared his throat discreetly. "Excuse me, Miss Ryan. I'm sorry to interrupt your dinner," he said, apologizing, "but there's a gentleman here who insists he must see you. I explained that you were at dinner, but he said he would only take a few minutes of your time."

"Who is this man?" Caitlin inquired.

"A Mr. Horton, ma'am."

"Avil Horton!" Jed burst out angrily. "What gall that man has!" Jed threw down his napkin. "I'll take care of him." Pushing his chair back, Jed stood up and glanced down at Caitlin, who was obviously concerned. "Don't worry, it'll only take a few minutes. I'll be right back."

"I think I should go, Jed. He did ask to see me. I can handle him."

"I *know* you could. But I have a feeling he's old school, and will listen to a man better."

Biting her lip, Caitlin agreed. "As long as you're not becoming a chauvinist, Jed Michaels. Oh, just get rid of him." She watched Jed leave. "What can that horrible man possibly hope to gain by coming here?"

"I don't know," Melanie said sympathetically. "From what you told me about his manager, he seems pretty determined to get Magic for himself. But I'm sure Jed can take care of him. Don't worry, Caitlin, it'll be all right."

"She's right," Howard said and looked at Caitlin with an encouraging smile. "And if Jed feels the need for a lawyer to back him up, I'm right here."

"And you couldn't ask for a better lawyer," Melanie said loyally.

"I know." Caitlin smiled distractedly and picked up her fork. "Let's not let this delicious swordfish go to waste."

Rollins had come back into the room and was picking up Jed's plate. "I'll just take Mr. Michaels's plate into the kitchen and see that it's kept warm until he returns."

"Oh, thank you, Rollins," Caitlin said.

After the butler had left with Jed's plate, she turned to Melanie and asked how she was enjoying her aerobics class. With a half-serious groan, Melanie gave Caitlin a full report.

After a few minutes, though, Caitlin realized that her attention had wandered. All she was thinking about was Jed and the confrontation in the other room. Abruptly she excused herself, saying, "I'm sorry, but I really have to see what's going on in there."

Approaching the closed doors to the library, Caitlin expected to hear heated voices coming

35

through the wood panels. But there wasn't a sound. When she opened one of the doors and stepped into the room, she saw Jed quietly speaking to a man with hawklike features and a thin mouth set in a straight line. Although it had been several years since Caitlin had last encountered Avil Horton, she instantly recalled the repulsion she had felt when he rudely cut in front of her to take a jump first.

Jed paused, glancing toward Caitlin as she entered the room. Avil Horton, too, looked in her direction.

"Ah, Miss Ryan," he said smoothly, addressing her with a slight nod of his head. "It's been some time since we last met. How good to see you again."

"Mr. Horton." Caitlin acknowledged him coolly before turning to Jed. "Are you two almost finished?" She looked back at Horton and said, "We were in the middle of dinner."

"Of course. I apologize for barging in like this," the older man said. "But I thought it best to come and speak to you tonight, before you went to the trouble of having Magic Man brought here." He smiled pleasantly. "You see, I was just explaining to Mr. Michaels here that the sale to you was a mistake. The horse was already spoken for, but unfortunately there was some kind of misunderstanding. I'm sorry for the inconven—"

"There was no mistake, Mr. Horton," Jed interrupted, looking straight at the older man. "I have already explained that we made the highest bid, and the horse was sold to us. I'm sorry, but that's that."

"Normally that would be true, but there was a gentleman's agreement involved," Horton told Caitlin. "Surely you, Miss Ryan, can understand that."

"Of course," Caitlin said smoothly. "I understand all too well—you made a pact with the auctioneer to buy Magic. But when we topped your final offer, the auctioneer had no choice but to sell the colt to us. If he hadn't, everyone would have known he was crooked. So you see, Mr. Horton, I know all about your *agreement*."

"Okay, how much do you want?" Horton asked. "I'll give you double what you paid: two million, two hundred thousand."

"That's a lot of money," Jed said.

"Yes, and you could do a lot with that much. You could buy several horses with as much potential as Magic Man."

"Why do you want him so badly?" Caitlin asked, taking a couple of steps farther into the room. "As you say, there are other horses available."

"Let's just say I've taken a liking to this particular colt. That's all the reason I need."

"Well, he's not for sale," Jed said quickly. "Not at any price."

Caitlin could see the expression in Horton's eyes as Jed spoke. It was cold—cold and determined.

"You're quite wrong there," he said to Jed. "*Everyone* has a price. Perhaps in this instance the price is not money. Perhaps it's something else. But whatever it is, I will discover it."

Caitlin felt a sudden shiver slide down her spine. She wanted that man out of her house. "You've said what you came here to say, Mr. Horton, now would you please leave?"

Taking the man's arm, Jed began to steer him toward the library door. But Horton disengaged himself from Jed's grasp. Brushing at the sleeve of his suit jacket, he said, "You've made yourselves perfectly clear. Perfectly clear."

A moment later, after their visitor had left, Caitlin leaned against Jed and sighed. "That man scares me."

"Caitlin, honey—" Jed said soothingly. "I don't want you to worry. We're not about to be intimidated by that snake." He tilted her chin up

38

so he could look into her eyes. "As I said this afternoon, his threats are just so much hot air. When his manager didn't succeed with us, he had to try himself."

"Jed, you don't know him," Caitlin said. "He's not just horrid on the hunt field, he has a terrible reputation in business as well. Avil Horton does not make hollow threats, I promise you that."

"Believe me," Jed said, tenderly kissing her forehead, "he can't hurt us. If he tries anything, we'll find a way to fight him—and win."

Caitlin remembered his words as she and Jed left the house the next morning and started across the broad, manicured back lawn. Looking lovely in form-fitting fawn breeches, polished boots, and a yellow turtleneck, she smiled up at Jed. "You were right about Avil Horton. He had me frightened last night, but I've been thinking, and I realize that he's just a rude man who won't take no for an answer."

"But he's going to have to," Jed said, agreeing.

"Right. Magic is really ours." She took his hand, and tugged. "Now come on, hurry. I want to make sure that everything is perfect at the stable when he arrives."

They were heading toward the new barn, which was being built to replace the barn that had burned several weeks before. Almost complete, the new stable was luxurious. There were thirty-two spacious stalls, a humidity-controlled feed room, a walnut-paneled tack room, and a large, comfortable office for Jed. From there, he planned to handle the business affairs of the new Ryan Acres Racing Stable.

Caitlin had also ordered the most technologically advanced security system available. Television cameras continuously swept over every foot of the building, and there were also sophisticated alarms on every door and window. She was determined that no one would ever harm her horses again. Thankfully, all the horses had been led out of the burning barn safely, and the only person who had been hurt was Howard. He had had his leg broken when a frightened horse trampled him. Howard was fine now, although he still sported a light cast. And, as he had told them at dinner the night before, he was going to insist that the doctor take it off before the wedding. "I don't think it would look right for the best man to hobble up to the altar in a cast," he had explained.

"Jed, did you get Magic's stall ready?" Caitlin asked.

"Yes." Jed smiled down at her. "Don't worry, everything is perfect. Early this morning I came down and talked with Jeff. We're giving Magic one of the corner stalls, the one closest to the large paddock. There's plenty of fresh straw for his bedding, and his high-protein hay is already in the feeder."

"What about water?" she asked, teasing him. "Did you check to make sure his drinking system works?"

"Yes, it's fine." Jed chuckled. Taking her hands in his, he squeezed them gently. "I'll have you know, Caitlin Ryan, that I even remembered to put a brand-new salt block in the holder next to the feeder. You see I can do some things on my own. I promise you, Magic is going to love it here—especially with you here to spoil him."

"I won't spoil him," she retorted, trying to sound indignant. She knew, though, that Jed was right.

"Oh, sure you will," he said with a laugh. "But you'd better not let me catch you feeding him sugar cubes and carrots. After all, he'll be an athlete in training."

"I know, I know," she said. "And I trust you to make sure that everything is just right. But you know me—I always have to see for myself."

"Yes, I guess you do." He grinned and said, "Lead on."

Lou Becker arrived just before the van carrying Magic Man came up the drive. Bending his tall, lanky frame, he unfolded himself out of his car and strode toward them. He held out his hand to Jed as he came closer.

"Hello, there. Looks as though I arrived just in time," he said, nodding toward the van. He turned and smiled at Caitlin, who immediately liked the middle-aged man. He had a strong face, with dark brown eyes and a long, thin nose. "And you must be Caitlin," he said as he shook her hand.

The three of them stood together outside the stable as the van came up the graveled drive and stopped in front of them. The driver got out, and soon the gray colt was being led down the ramp. Jeff, the head stable man, took the lead and brought him prancing over to Jed and Caitlin so they could inspect him. He was dressed for travel in a blanket and protective headgear, and his legs had been wrapped to guard against bruising bumps.

"May I?" Lou asked, glancing at Jed and Caitlin. Jed nodded. Lou quickly stripped the blanket and other gear off the yearling. Then he ran his hands over the colt's shining coat and down each leg. Standing up straight, he smiled. "Looks like he made the trip nicely."

"So, what do you think of him?" Caitlin asked.

"Well, I've seen him before, as you know," Lou replied. "I try to keep an eye on every yearling that shows potential." He motioned toward Magic Man. "This guy certainly has it, too—with a capital *P*." He shoved his hands into the pockets of his jeans and rocked back and forth on the balls of his feet. "To be honest, I'm glad you're giving me the chance to train him. I think I'm the man who can get the best out of him."

"Then you'll take him on?" Jed asked. Lou nodded. "I like a man who's confident and makes up his mind quickly." He glanced toward Jeff, who was attempting to keep the colt still but not having much luck. Magic Man was obviously full of energy. "Why don't you walk him around a bit, Jeff? Let him stretch his legs."

The stable man nodded. As Jeff led the snorting colt away, Jed turned again to Lou. "Would you like to go into the office where the three of us can talk?"

"Or perhaps the house?" Caitlin said. "I could have Margaret bring us some iced tea out on the terrace."

"Thank you, but right here's just fine." He looked at Jed and said, "You mentioned something about putting in some training facilities—a practice starting gate, perhaps even a full track." He glanced around. "What exactly did you have in mind, and where will you put it?"

"Well, we want to put in a track right over here," Jed replied, walking toward a pasture fence. The other two followed.

"Caitlin and I have talked about it," Jed said, leaning an elbow on the top rail. "And we decided that if we're going into the racing business, we should do it the right way."

"I agree," Lou replied. "I much prefer training a horse on the owner's property. The security's often better, and not everyone knows how he's coming along." He stopped for a moment, then motioned toward the broad, flat pasture. "I know a guy who can design and put in a track for you. He's good. And if you get it started soon, it should be ready by the time Magic Man is ready for track work."

Jed nodded. "Tell your friend to give me a call, and we can set up an appointment."

"Fine, I'll do that." Lou pushed himself away from the fence, and the three began walking back toward his car. "I'd like to have the colt— uh, Magic—spend the next week just resting up. The sale and settling into a new place can be a bit stressful for a Thoroughbred."

"We'll make sure he gets his rest," Caitlin said as a promise.

"I'll come over a week from tomorrow and get him started on his serious training."

"We'll be on our honeymoon by then," Jed said. "But I'll leave instructions with Jeff that you're to be given every courtesy."

"Thank you. And congratulations," Lou said heartily. He stopped in front of his car. "When you get back, we can talk about which races we should put him in to condition him for the Dogwood Cup. And perhaps we can talk about hiring a jockey. It may be a bit early, but I like to plan ahead."

"Then you really think he can run in the Dogwood Cup?" Caitlin asked eagerly.

"Oh, absolutely, Miss Ryan," Lou told her. "Not only run, but win."

4

The next few days were busy ones for Caitlin. They were frantic but happy, filled with last-minute wedding details. As she told Melanie on Thursday morning, while the two were unwrapping the latest wedding presents, "I'm so glad I've got you here to help me out. I don't know how I'd make it without you." She held out the present she had just opened. "Can you believe it? A set of twelve pickle forks!"

With a grin, Melanie picked up one of the tiny sterling silver forks and looked at it with raised eyebrows. "I don't know, Caitlin, maybe pickles have become really popular. Maybe in some circles every dinner guest needs his or her own pickle fork."

Caitlin nodded wryly and searched through

the wrapping paper for the card. "They're from Dean and Susan, friends of my father. I'll have to think of something nice to write on the thank-you note."

"It may be tough," Melanie said as she handed Caitlin another silver-ribboned package. "Here, open this one. Maybe it's a set of twelve finger bowls!"

Jed had made sure that he was away from the house as much as possible that week. He spent most of his time at the stable—either in his office or in the pasture with the men who were preparing the land for the new track.

Caitlin went down to visit Jed whenever she could get away. But Peggy Scott, the woman Caitlin had hired to oversee the wedding, kept her very busy.

Now that the lawn tent was to be yellow and white, Caitlin and Peggy had decided that yellow should be the dominant color scheme for the entire affair. The tent was already up, and surrounding it like a flotilla of small boats were twenty-five white tables topped with bright yellow umbrellas that had been sent by overnight mail from New York only the day before. Dwarf lemon trees in white planters would be massed everywhere, and vases overflowing with

47

roses, freesias, lilies, and pale yellow gladioluses would be set on the long, narrow serving tables and individual tables.

Caitlin finally left Peggy and Rollins arguing about where to put several cases of champagne and walked down to the barns to see Jed.

When she arrived, he was on the phone, so she opened his door and let him know she was there. Then she went on to Magic Man's stall.

As she stroked the velvety skin of the colt's muzzle, she suddenly realized she hadn't even thought of Avil Horton and his threats since Sunday. It was now Thursday. She smiled to herself, then murmured to Magic Man, "Jed was right. That man is just a big, old windbag. You're safe here with us." As if he understood, Magic Man nickered softly and bumped her hand with his head.

The sound of Jed slamming down the phone startled her, and Caitlin turned to watch him stride toward her. He looked absolutely furious.

"What is it, Jed? What's wrong?" Sensing trouble, Magic Man had turned and was now standing at the back of his stall. Caitlin wished she could be there, too.

"My mother, that's what's wrong!" Jed announced bitterly.

"Your mother?" Caitlin said, taken aback.

The last time Jed had heard from his mother was just after his father's death a few years earlier. He hadn't heard from her directly, but from her attorney, who had written to say she wanted to sell the family ranch, which had been left to her in Mr. Michaels's will.

Jed's mother had run away to Hollywood to live with a movie producer she had met while he was filming a movie near their ranch in Montana. Neither Jed nor Melanie had seen her since their early teens, and she had never written or called.

"Can you believe it?" Jed shook his head. "She wanted to come to the wedding."

Caitlin stared at him. "But—how did she even know about it?"

"In Suzie Saint Clair's column," he said. "I guess they run it in one of the L.A. papers."

"Oh." Caitlin was silent for a moment. "Well, what did you tell her?"

"I said no, of course." He sighed, shaking his head. "But she just kept insisting, saying how sorry she was that she left me and Melanie, how she realizes now that she was wrong, and how she wants to make up for all that lost time. As if that were really possible."

"Jed, I'm sorry," Caitlin said softly. Her heart went out to him, but at the same time she felt sorry for Mrs. Michaels, too. The woman had made a mistake, a terrible mistake, in leaving her children, but now she was trying to make up for it. Didn't she at least deserve a chance?

"She says she wants to meet you," Jed said. "She said she wants to get to know her new daughter-in-law. As if she had the right to—"

"Be human?" Caitlin said, finishing the sentence for him. "I know how much she hurt you, but maybe it's time to forgive her. I have the feeling she's always loved you."

"She sure has had a funny way of showing it. Not so much as a birthday card, a call, nothing! I never heard from her once in all those years."

"Maybe she thought your father wouldn't want her to get in touch with you. Or maybe she was afraid to call after she left the way she did."

"Forget it, Caitlin! I don't want anything to do with her. She's out of my life, out of our lives. You said it—she left. *She* made the choice, and now she'll have to live with it." Running his hand through his wavy hair, Jed sighed. He looked back at Caitlin and smiled slightly. "Case closed, okay?" Taking her hand, he added, "Now, come on outside. I want to show you where we've decided to put the practice starting gate."

* * *

The morning of Jed and Caitlin's wedding was cloudless and bright. The temperature was to be in the seventies. The ceremony was set for eleven-thirty, with a wedding lunch afterward.

By seven o'clock, Caitlin was dressed and downstairs in the kitchen. She managed to drink part of a cup of coffee, but couldn't even think of eating. Finally she went to look for Peggy, who was to have arrived at the house by six that morning in order to orchestrate the final details.

Caitlin found her in a beige suit in the living room. She was busy directing where to place a bank of ferns and white roses against a marble fireplace.

The green and peach furniture that normally filled the beautiful room had been brought up to the second floor the day before. Now rows of rented folding chairs filled the room, waiting for the guests to arrive. The bank of ferns and roses was being set up in front, to serve as the backdrop for the minister. As Caitlin walked up the aisle toward Peggy, she couldn't help but think that in only a few hours she would be standing there saying her vows. *It's really true,* she thought. *Jed and I are going to be married.*

Just as Caitlin reached the front of the room, Peggy turned around. "Good morning. How are you feeling? Nervous?"

51

"Not a bit," Caitlin said, assuring the older woman. "How are we doing down here?"

"Everything is fine and on schedule," Peggy reported. "The catering crew is in the kitchen, the champagne is on ice, and the serving help will arrive"—she looked at her watch—"in about an hour and a half. As you requested, I've hired three college kids to park cars, so there shouldn't be any trouble there."

"What about the security people?"

"They're already in place—very discreetly. They've done the best weddings. They have the guest list, as well as the names of the members of the press who will be permitted on the estate. None of the press, of course, will be allowed to attend the actual ceremony or the reception. They'll have to get their pictures and stories from a distance."

"Good." Caitlin nodded. "I would rather not have the press at all, but I suppose it can't be helped."

"You are a rather well-known person," Peggy said with an understanding smile. "Why, there must be hundreds of young women who would give almost anything to change places with you."

Caitlin had heard such compliments before, but they still embarrassed her. She wanted to giggle at the thought of photographers sneaking around the bushes trying to get a picture of her in her wedding dress. Instead, though, she smiled politely, then changed the subject.

"Well, I'm glad to hear that everything's under control. Did you ever think you'd get it all done?" Both women smiled. Taking a step backward, Caitlin said happily, "Now if you'll excuse me, I have to start getting ready."

Hurrying back down the hall toward the stairs, she passed the open doors of the library and heard Jed yelling.

Oh, no, she thought, recalling the phone call from his mother earlier. Why did she have to call again? And on the morning of their wedding, too. Caitlin stepped closer, listening to Jed's side of the conversation.

"Your problem is that you don't understand the meaning of the word no, Mr. Horton!"

Horton? A picture of the dreadful man, standing in the library the previous Saturday evening, flashed into her mind. Despite the pleasantly warm morning, she felt herself shiver.

Going into the library, she saw Jed standing behind the desk, an angry scowl on his face. Seeing Caitlin enter, he pointed to the mouthpiece and shook his head in disgust.

She nodded her understanding and went to stand near him.

"I'll only tell you this one more time, Horton," Jed said. "And I suggest you listen this time." He paused for a moment for emphasis. "We are definitely *not* interested in selling Magic Man. Not to you, not to anyone. Threaten us all you want, he's not for sale."

Caitlin nodded her agreement, then looked up at Jed again.

"For your information," Jed replied, "we've already entered him in the Dogwood Cup. And what's more, we expect him to win."

That time she could hear Horton answering. She couldn't make out all the words, but it was obvious they weren't polite ones. The muscles along Jed's jaw tightened, and then he finally said, "Goodbye, and don't ever call again." Jed slammed the phone down. "That man makes me so mad!" he said, exploding.

"What did he say?" Caitlin looked at him, worried.

Taking a deep breath, he forced himself to calm down. He took Caitlin's hands in his and said, "I'm sorry. I wish you hadn't heard that. Look, it's really nothing. The guy's just being unpleasant, that's all."

"You're not fooling me," she replied, studying

his face. "What did Horton really say? You know I don't like secrets, not even when you're trying to protect me from someone like that man. Was he making more threats?"

"All right, I'll tell you." Jed grimaced. "He warned us not to enter Magic Man in any races. I guess you heard me tell him that we already had." Caitlin nodded. "He said we were making a mistake by doing that, a big mistake."

"What are we going to do?" Caitlin asked.

"Don't worry," Jed said, putting his arms around her and pulling her close. "Let's not let that creep spoil the most wonderful day of our lives." He kissed her forehead tenderly. "He's just trying to scare us."

"He's dangerous," Caitlin said. She pulled her head back so she could look up into Jed's eyes. "I know he is. I feel it."

"That's exactly what he would like you to believe," Jed replied. "Because then you'll give in and sell Magic to him."

"Never!" she replied defiantly. "I'd never allow that horrid man to get his hands on Magic."

"Good girl," Jed said with a pleased smile. "Now you just remember that. Because no one's ever going to take Magic away from us."

"Are you really sure, Jed?"

"Positive." Grinning at her, he drew her closer to him. "Why don't you just forget Avil Horton even exists, and go upstairs and get ready. We have a wedding to go to."

Leaning down, he kissed her tenderly. When they parted, he murmured into her ear, "The next time we do that you'll be my wife."

The pianist had just started playing Pachelbel's Canon in D, and everyone turned to look at Caitlin. Ahead of her, proceeding down the aisle, were Melanie and her bridesmaids.

"Ready?" her father whispered.

Feeling a nervous flutter in her stomach, Caitlin smiled up at her father. "Yes, I'm ready." Resting her hand lightly on her father's arm, she started down the aisle. In keeping with tradition, she was wearing something "old," a strand of pearls that had belonged to her mother, and something "new," her wedding dress. The blue lace garter Emily had worn at her own wedding and lent to Caitlin covered "something borrowed and something blue." As she took another step, she felt the shiny new penny that Peggy had slipped into her white brocade shoe for luck just minutes before she came down the stairs.

Caitlin felt like a princess in a fairy tale. From

the moment she had first tried on her dress, she knew it was perfect for her. Made of ivory satin, it was lavishly trimmed in lace. A fine pink satin ribbon had been threaded through the lace that bordered the neckline and the fitted sleeves, giving it just a hint of color. The bodice of the dress fit tightly, emphasizing Caitlin's slim figure. The skirt ended in a chapel-length train. In her hands Caitlin carried a small spray of white baby orchids and a book of poems that had belonged to her mother.

Smiling, Caitlin wondered what Jed was thinking as he watched her walk down the aisle. Had this moment been worth waiting for? She hoped so. She hoped he would remember every detail of it for the rest of his life. She knew she would.

Jed was wearing a morning coat, a soft gray vest, and dark trousers. In his lapel there was a single champagne rose. But it was the expression on his face that took Caitlin's breath away. His laughing green eyes were filled with love, and the crooked smile she had always loved made her heart skip a beat.

I truly am the luckiest woman in the world, she thought as she and her father came to the end of the aisle. Dr. Westlake stepped back as Jed moved to her side. There was a hush as the music softly died away and the ceremony began. "Dearly beloved . . ."

To Caitlin, the entire ceremony went by in a haze. She was so nervous about getting everything right that she nearly forgot to hand Melanie her flowers when they came to the part where she and Jed exchanged rings. Finally, though, she remembered, and Jed slipped the circlet of tiny diamonds set in gold on her finger. Then it was her turn. Taking Jed's hand, she slipped the wide gold ring onto his finger, panicking only slightly when, for a moment, it wouldn't go over his knuckle. Moments later, the whole thing was over.

"I now pronounce you husband and wife. You may kiss the bride."

Jed turned and, lifting her veil, kissed her. Caitlin heard the minister politely clear his throat before Jed broke away and turned with her to start back up the aisle. "Didn't I say," he whispered as they walked, "that the next time I did that you'd be my wife?"

"And you're my husband."

As they reached the end of the aisle, everyone crowded around them to offer their congratulations. Caitlin's father shook Jed's hand, welcoming him into the family. The quartet began playing while Rollins and the other servants opened the french doors so that everyone could begin to make their way out onto the lawn, where the tent was set up.

The next two hours went by in a happy blur. Caitlin barely tasted the wedding luncheon of veal in apricot sauce with braised artichoke hearts and baby vegetables. She did remember someone taking a picture of her as she fed Jed a piece of the five-tier wedding cake, which was decorated with yellow and white sugar roses. Then came the dancing. For the first dance, Jed and Caitlin had asked the band to play "Stand by Me."

While the guests continued to dance and the waiters passed among them with fresh glasses of champagne, Caitlin and Jed sneaked away to change to leave on their honeymoon.

Melanie went with Caitlin to help her. Slipping out of her lovely dress, Caitlin changed into her going-away outfit—a yellow linen suit. She brushed the mass of curls out of her hair, then pulled it back into a casual ponytail. She paused to glance around the room, feeling a sudden wave of sadness. "It's kind of hard to believe that this is no longer my bedroom," she said to Melanie. "That when Jed and I get back, we'll be sharing our new suite."

"Umm-hmm." Melanie nodded. "I think I

know how you feel. It was like when I stood in my bedroom at the ranch for the last time. I knew my life had changed, and it would never be the same again." She walked over and put an arm around Caitlin's shoulders. "But your life is changing for all the right reasons. The *best* reasons."

"You're absolutely right," Caitlin said. Then she hugged Melanie. "How did I ever get such a sensible, understanding sister-in-law?"

"Luck, I guess." Melanie laughed at her own immodesty. Then, in a more solemn tone, she said, "And as your sister-in-law, I have new responsibilities. One of them is to get you back to Jed so that you can make that plane on time." Counting on her fingers, she reeled off the plan. "Jed has the tickets—Howard made sure of that. Rollins should have the Bentley pulled around in front by now, and I know—because I checked myself—that your luggage as well as Jed's is in the trunk." She grinned and picked up Caitlin's small bouquet. "And last but certainly not least, I will go tell everyone that you are about ready to throw your bouquet." She started to hand Caitlin the orchids, then pulled back. "You do remember who you're supposed to aim for, don't you?"

"But I have to turn my back to throw it,"

Caitlin objected. Then, smiling, she added, "I'll try to aim for you."

"Good. Here are your flowers." She handed them to Caitlin and was gone.

Alone, Caitlin took one last look around. She picked up a photograph in a silver frame from her bedside table. It was a picture of her mother, a mother she had never known. She had died when Caitlin was born. But Caitlin was sure that her mother had been there that day, as had her grandmother, Regina Ryan.

Picking up her purse and holding the white ribboned spray of orchids, she left her room.

5

Caitlin turned over onto her stomach and rested her head on her arms, digging her toes into the warm sand. There wasn't a cloud in sight, but the flower-scented breeze kept the tropical sun from feeling too hot on her bare shoulders.

"Ummmm," she murmured contentedly.

"Happy?" Jed asked from beside her. His voice was drowsy. Looking over at her new husband, she saw that his eyes were closed. His normally light brown eyelashes looked almost blond in contrast to the dark tan he had gotten in the past nine days.

"Very," she said, closing her own eyes. "I think I could stay here forever."

They were lying on the beach by the gentle Kahana Bay on the windward side of Oahu.

After spending the day snorkeling in the shallow aquamarine water, they had eaten a picnic lunch that had been packed for them by the hotel chef. The narrow beach was peaceful and quiet, a place where very few tourists visited.

Opening her eyes again, Caitlin sat up and leaned on her elbows. She looked around her at the beautiful emerald green hills that rose up around the quiet patch of water. "I wish we didn't have to go home the day after tomorrow," she said.

"Me, too," Jed answered. Rolling over to face her, he drew hearts in the sand with his finger. "Wouldn't it be great if we could stay here forever?"

"Maybe we could come back again soon."

"Yeah, real soon." Leaning closer, he kissed the tip of her nose. "How about next month?"

"Sure." Caitlin laughed happily.

Jed nuzzled her neck. "Mmm, you smell wonderful. What's the name of that perfume you bought on Kauai?"

"It's called *pikake*."

"It smells like that stuff you wear at home," he said as he kissed the hollow of her collar bone.

"Jasmine," she said, poking his ankle with her bare foot. "Don't you remember? The saleslady said *pikake* is the Hawaiian word for jasmine."

"Oh, yeah." The tone of Jed's voice made it obvious that he wasn't really listening. Trailing kisses along her neck, he pulled her into his arms. Then, looking searchingly into her eyes, he started tickling her.

"Jed, stop that!" she cried. She wriggled away, still laughing, and scrambled over to the far side of the blanket. In a breathless voice, she said, "You are the meanest, most horrible husband—"

"Oh, I am, am I?" Jed made a face at her, then smiled. Getting to his feet, he reached down and pulled her up, too. "If you want mean, I'll show you mean," he said, a twinkle in his eye. Without letting go of her hand, he raced down the beach toward the ocean and jumped in. As the water splashed over her warm skin, Caitlin squealed and tried to pull away. But Jed kept going until the water was hip high. Then he gathered her into his arms and plunged backward into the water.

A moment later they surfaced, both laughing and gasping for breath. Still holding her in his arms, Jed kissed her tenderly.

That evening they ate at a Japanese restaurant, where the chef prepared dinner before their eyes at a grill set into the table. The cooking was really a form of entertainment, with the flashing of sharp knives and the precise rows of sliced meat and brightly colored vegetables.

After dinner they decided to go dancing and ended up at the Summit. It was located at the top of the Ala Moana Hotel, and from there they could look out over the lights of Honolulu. As they moved together to the romantic strains of Hawaiian guitars, Caitlin rested her head against Jed's chest. The next day was to be their last full day in Hawaii, she thought sadly. But then she smiled, thinking of all the exciting things they had already done. There didn't seem to be all that much left for them to try.

They had gone hiking, snorkeling, and even skin diving. But Caitlin knew that Jed's favorite had been the surfing. He had introduced the sport to her at a beach in Maui where the waves were especially tame. Even so, Caitlin had been scared half to death. Surfing was one sport Jed could pursue by himself.

Looking back, it seemed as if the only places they hadn't visited were the Buddhist temple and Chinatown—and they had missed seeing the U.S.S. Arizona National Memorial at Pearl Harbor. But none of those tourist attractions seemed special enough for their last day. *We really should do something to make it a day to remember,* Caitlin thought.

"Jed?" She looked up at him.

"Tired of dancing?"

"Never," she replied, shaking her head slightly. "No, I was just thinking that we never decided what to do tomorrow."

"Oh, yeah, right." Jed hesitated. "Well, actually, I did think of a place I'd like to go, something I'd like to do."

"Really? What?"

He grinned. "I'd like to see if I can surf the Banzai Pipeline."

"Oh, Jed, look at those waves! Please tell me you aren't serious about going out in them," Caitlin said as Jed helped her from the car the next morning.

After breakfast they had driven to the Kahana side of Oahu, away from Honolulu. Now, staring out at the ocean, Caitlin felt a knot of fear form a tight ball in her stomach. *Jed could kill himself trying to surf out there*, she thought.

Never had she ever seen such frighteningly powerful waves. They crashed in and curled over upon themselves one right after another. Some were as high as a two-story building, and they moved with tremendous force and speed. As they curled, they formed a tunnel of fast-moving dark green water.

Caitlin shivered involuntarily as she pictured Jed falling off his board and being lost beneath the pounding surf.

"You bet I'm going out," Jed replied. He, too, had been staring out at the waves, the excitement of the challenge was building inside him. He didn't seem to realize that Caitlin was terrified. "I can hardly wait."

"Jed—" she said, putting her hand on his arm to stop him. "I don't want you to surf here."

"But, Caitlin, that's the Pipeline. It's a surfer's dream to ride that." He pointed toward the water. "Look at those guys out there. Do they look scared?"

"Jed, they look like they surf here all the time. They're probably used to it. If you want to surf so badly, why don't we go back to Waikiki? You liked it when we surfed there the other day."

"Waikiki!" Jed shook his head. "That's not real surfing. That's for beginners and old ladies."

"Well, all I know is that *I* had a tough time staying up," she said.

"Yeah," he said, nodding. "That's because you're a beginner. And I had fun there because I was teaching you. But I'm not a beginner. If you'll remember, I've been surfing for almost three years, and I think I know my way around a board."

"Yes, I'm sure you do," she replied, feeling the coolness creep into her voice. "But not in waves like those." She jerked her head toward the crashing surf. "Jed, it's foolish to take the kind of chance those guys out there are taking. They're pros and you're not." She looked into his eyes for a hint that he was weakening. When she didn't see one, she tried a different approach. "Jed, if I mean anything to you, if you care even the slightest bit how I feel, you won't do this. Please, Jed!" She could see the tenseness around Jed's mouth, the tightening of the skin at the corners of his eyes—but she couldn't stop herself. She loved him, and she didn't want him going out there—no matter what. "Anything could happen out there."

"Caitlin," he said, the coolness in his voice more than matching hers, "you don't have to remind me of the dangers of surfing. I'm fully aware of them."

"But—" She had lost, and she knew it. She loved him so much, yet they were on the verge of a real argument. It would be terrible to end their honeymoon that way. And maybe she was letting her fears run away with her. After all, Jed wasn't dumb. She wouldn't have fallen in love with him, married him, if he was. So why didn't she trust his judgment? She pasted a smile on her face, and said, "I'm sorry, Jed. I didn't mean to say those things. It's just that I love you so very much. I waited so long to be married to you, and I guess I just want to make sure nothing bad ever happens to you."

"I think we both know you can't do that," Jed answered. He smiled, and as he did the tension left his face. He put his arm around her waist and gave her a little hug. "And neither of us would be happy if you tried."

She nodded and slid both her arms around him. "I think we just had our first married fight."

"Do you want to divorce me?" Jed asked in a teasing tone.

"Only if it happens again. Now get out there and surf."

"I promise," he said seriously, "that I'll be very careful out there. And we won't stay long. Then we'll go back over to Honolulu and have lunch at that sushi bar you liked."

Caitlin took a deep breath to get rid of the fear she still felt as she watched Jed walk to the palm-roofed shelter where a man was renting surfboards. As she got her beach mat and tote out of the car, she remembered with relief that the next day they would be heading back to Ryan Acres. And there wouldn't be any more surfing to worry about for a long time.

6

As soon as they returned from Hawaii, Caitlin was back at her desk in the library at Ryan Acres, working. She wanted to catch up on everything as quickly as possible. Reading over a report that Randolph Woods had dropped off earlier, she quickly became drawn into the company's problems again.

After successfully fighting Colin Wollman's attempt to destroy the company, Caitlin had decided to stay on as president of Ryan Mining. But she only went into the office two or three times a week, preferring to do as much work as possible from home. Fortunately, in addition to being a good attorney, Randolph Woods had also turned out to be someone whose judgment she could trust and rely upon.

The report Caitlin was reading turned out to be a pleasant surprise. It said that the renovation of some old and out-of-date equipment in the mine at Rock Ridge had finally been completed. Now the mine ranked among the safest in the country. A new work schedule had also been drawn up and approved by the miners' union. Everyone hoped that the shorter shifts would minimize the danger of accident caused by tired workers.

Picking up a pen, she signed the space on the last page to show that she had read and approved the report. She was putting the top back on her pen when she heard a soft knock on the door.

Looking up, she saw Jed standing in the doorway. He was unbearably handsome in Levis, boots, and a flannel shirt with the sleeves rolled up. He ran a hand through his sun-streaked hair, and looked back at her shyly, as if he still felt out of place in the middle of such luxury. Caitlin felt her heart melt.

"Hi, there," he said. "Looks as though my timing is just about perfect. All through for the morning?"

"Ummm—yes," Caitlin said as she stretched lazily. Then she noticed a funny expression on Jed's face. There was a sort of mischievous look in his green eyes. "What do you mean, your timing's perfect?"

"Oh, nothing. I just thought you might like to have lunch with me—a nice, long lunch," he said, his voice teasing now. "I had Mrs. Crowley fix us something a little special."

"Special? What?"

"I'm not telling." With a grin, he crossed the room and pulled her to her feet. "So what do you say? Can Ryan Mining do without you for the afternoon?"

"Now it's the whole afternoon?" she asked, her eyebrows raised.

"Well, we'll see how it goes."

"And what about Ryan Acres business?" she countered.

"Running smoothly, thank you." He kissed the tip of her nose. "Now, are you hungry?"

She laughed. "Actually, I'm starved. It seems like it's been hours since breakfast."

"It has. You've been in here since eight, and it's almost one now." He led her away from the desk. "You know what they say about people who are all work and no play."

"They're dull?" She tipped her head to look up at him, smiling.

"That's right. And I don't want you becoming dull."

73

In the hall Caitlin started to turn toward the dining room, but Jed shook his head. Taking her hand, he led her toward the broad, curving staircase.

"I said *special*," Jed said.

A minute later he opened the door to the master bedroom. Caitlin saw that the small table in the lovely bay window where they sometimes ate breakfast was set with crisp white linen, crystal, and silver. In the center, between tall white candles, was a vase of pink roses—her favorite. Beside the table stood a silver wine bucket with a bottle of champagne cooling in it. Finally she noticed a tiny package, tied with an enormous pink bow, sitting on one of the plates.

"But—" She turned to him, her mouth open in surprise.

"Happy anniversary, honey."

"Oh, Jed!" Her hand flew to her mouth.

"It's one month today."

"You remembered and I forgot," she said, letting her hand fall away. "Oh, Jed, how absolutely adorable of you to think of this." She walked toward the table. Turning to face him again, she shook her head. "I feel terrible. I didn't get you anything."

"I just wanted to make you happy." He went

to stand beside her. "It definitely was a surprise, huh?"

"Yes, it sure was," she answered as tears of happiness glistened in her eyes.

"Hey, don't cry." He wiped away the one tear that had spilled over the dark fringe of her lashes. "See, the way I have it figured," he explained, "is that when I mess up and forget our real anniversary, you'll remember today and forgive me."

"Ah, so that's your strategy." She laughed happily, reaching up to hold his strong chin between her two slender hands. "That's very smart of you." Standing on tiptoe, she kissed him. "You're forgiven in advance, then."

"Hmmm, I almost feel like skipping lunch," he said. "However, I don't think Mrs. Crowley would appreciate that. She really did go to a lot of trouble over this lunch." He went over to a rolling tea cart, and lifted domed silver covers to show her delicate cheese crepes with truffles and asparagus tips and minted melon balls. And, for dessert, the cook had made Caitlin's favorite, white chocolate mousse. "There's some caviar here, too. How about a little, with the champagne, of course?"

Opening the wine, he filled a glass, then handed it to her. Pouring a glass for himself, he held it up in a toast. "To you, Caitlin, my beautiful wife. I love you more than words can say."

"Oh, Jed," Caitlin whispered. The moment was almost too wonderful to bear.

"All right," he said, putting his glass down. "You have to open this now." He picked up the expertly wrapped package and handed it to her. "I got it the day after we got back from Hawaii. Ever since then, I've been dying to give it to you." He paused, a flash of concern crossing his face. "I hope you like it."

"I'm sure I'm going to absolutely adore whatever it is," she replied automatically as she ripped away the wrapping paper. Inside a white cardboard box, there was a velvet jeweler's box. Caitlin took a deep breath and gently opened the lid. She gasped when she saw what lay inside on the tiny pillow of white satin. "Oh, Jed—it's gorgeous. Please." She held out the box to him. "Put it on for me."

Jed lifted the finely wrought platinum chain and charm from the box and fastened it around Caitlin's slim neck. "There," he said. "What do you think?"

Looking at her reflection in the mirror above her dresser, Caitlin reached up to touch the tiny charm. It was a miniature replica of the rose emblem that adorned the new Ryan Acres racing silks. The stem was made of platinum, the leaves were emeralds, and the initials and rose were both amethysts.

"I'll never take it off," she murmured blissfully. "Never." Turning in Jed's arms, she whispered, "Thank you, my darling. It's the most perfect gift anyone has ever given me."

By mid-October the practice track was nearly complete. A professional-quality four-horse starting gate had been delivered to the estate and was ready to be wheeled into place as soon as the final grading was finished and the turf laid down.

"Not a minute too soon, either," Lou Becker told Jed as they strolled away from the track where they had been watching the workers put up the outside rail. The inside rail had been finished the day before, and another two-man crew was putting on the first coat of white paint. "Magic is really coming along very well," Lou said. "Faster than a lot of colts I've trained."

"I'm glad to hear that," Jed replied.

"In fact, I think I can even start legging him up next week. We'll need the track for that, but fortunately, as I said, it's almost ready."

Jed looked a bit confused. "What exactly do you mean by 'legging him up'?"

"Oh, I'm sorry," the trainer said. "That's what we term the start of a horse's real training on the track. There's a little slow riding at first, then some light galloping to strengthen his muscles and start building up his wind."

"Oh, I see." Jed ran a hand over his hair as his mouth curved up in a grin. "I'm really looking forward to seeing this guy run. And Caitlin hasn't been able to talk about anything else ever since we bought him."

"Well, he won't be doing any really fast running at first," Lou said. "A horse that young has to be brought along slowly to prevent any injuries to his legs." He stuck his hands into the pockets of his jeans and looked at Jed thoughtfully. "I don't think it's smart to try to push things."

"Oh, no," Jed said, agreeing. "Caitlin and I want only what's best for Magic."

"Good." Lou nodded. "We're in agreement there."

They entered the stable. During the past week, Lou had been working the yearling out in one of the paddocks, having him circle around on a long lead called a longe line. He had also been getting Magic Man used to wearing a saddle and a bridle. Now the colt was being rubbed down and groomed before being put into his stall and fed his evening meal. The trainer wanted to take one final look at him before leaving for the day.

Immediately after he and Caitlin had gotten home from their honeymoon, Jed had hired an extra stable boy, someone to look after Magic almost exclusively. Jeff, the head stable man, had recommended Johnny Carns, saying he'd known the boy a long time and that he and his wife were friends of Johnny's whole family.

"This is the perfect job for him," Jeff had told Jed. "He's honest, and he'll take good care of the colt. He loves horses, especially racehorses. Besides, his mother would be terribly grateful if you could give Johnny a job here."

"Why is that?" Jed questioned.

"Oh, because she feels he's been hanging around over at Mac Johnson's stable too much. She thinks the stable hands there are a bit on the rough side, and she's afraid he'll get in with the wrong crowd." Jeff gave Jed a knowing look. "She's right, too, Mr. Michaels. Johnny's a good kid, a real hard worker. He won't be getting into trouble here, I'll promise you that."

Jeff's assurance had been good enough for Jed. After a brief interview, during which he noticed how well Johnny got along with Magic Man, he told the young man the job was his if he wanted it.

Now, as Jed walked with Lou down the aisle to where Johnny was smoothing a body brush over Magic Man's shining dappled coat, Jed felt even more sure that he'd done the right thing. Johnny's love for Magic Man was obvious from the soothing way he talked to the horse as he worked.

The two men paused, watching as Johnny finished with the brush, then began to wind padded, supportive bandages around the colt's lower legs.

"There're a couple of other things I want to mention," the trainer said casually, studying Magic Man as Johnny wrapped and fastened the first bandage. "I think it's time we started thinking about choosing a jockey to ride for Ryan Acres. It's not too soon, you know."

"Really? Do you have anyone in mind?" Jed asked, absently stroking Magic Man's neck.

"Actually, yes. A guy named Red Meyers. I ran into him just the other day in town. He said he'd heard I was training Magic Man. Said he'd love to have the chance to ride such a beautiful horse." Lou shook his head, chuckling. "I almost thought he wanted to ask me if I'd hire him to be Magic's jockey, but he was too shy. Isn't that crazy? Imagine Red Meyers, shy." Lou laughed again.

"I'm afraid I don't know him," Jed said. "But tell me about him. Do you think he'd be good for Magic? And, more important, I guess, do you think he'd be available?"

Lou nodded. "I do think he and Magic would get along. Magic's a smart horse, but I've noticed he's got a bit of a mind of his own. He's going to need a strong jockey, one who's got the guts to ride him. Red certainly has guts. I admire the way he handles a horse." Johnny had finished wrapping Magic Man's legs and was putting on his blanket. "As for him being available, that I don't know," Lou said. "But I'll give him a call and check it out. I should know by tomorrow afternoon. If he's free, I could set up an interview for you."

"Great, I'd appreciate that," Jed replied. He gave Magic Man a final pat. Lou, obviously satisfied with Johnny's work and the way Magic Man looked, gave the young man a nod of approval. Then he turned, ready to leave. "G'night, Johnny," he said.

"Good night, Mr. Becker," Johnny replied. Frowning, he watched the two men walk down the corridor and out of the stable.

"Red Meyers, huh," he muttered as he unhooked the cross ties, snapped the lead onto the ring of Magic Man's halter, and led him into his stall.

He grew angrier as he unsnapped the lead and filled the grain box. Stroking the horse's silky neck as the colt eagerly nosed into the oats, Johnny said, "I've heard bad things about Red Meyers. Very bad things. But, I guess, he couldn't be all that bad if Mr. Becker likes him. Maybe I'm wrong," he told Magic Man. "But I don't think so." He knew he was right because he had heard it from guys who should know, guys who wouldn't repeat stories like the ones he had heard unless they were true. Johnny let out an unhappy sigh.

As if he understood Johnny's problem, Magic Man stopped eating long enough to raise his head and look at the boy.

"Well, don't you worry, boy," Johnny said firmly. "I'll keep an eye out for that guy. No one's going to hurt you while I'm around. That's a promise."

As Magic Man went back to eating again, Johnny had a happy thought. "Hey, maybe it's not as bad as I thought," he told the colt, scratching behind his ear. "Mr. Michaels is a real smart man. He'll probably see right through that Red Meyers and tell him to get lost."

But two days later Johnny happened to be in the tack room and overheard Jed talking to Jeff. "Well, it looks like we have a jockey to ride our horse," he said. "I just hired Red Meyers."

7

Caitlin studied her reflection in the full-length mirror in her dressing room, trying to see if there was anything noticeably different about her. She turned sideways, eyeing herself critically. No, she decided, she looked the same as she always did.

Looking back at her from the mirror was a beautiful, slim young woman, and that was all. She smoothed down the front of her pleated pants, looking for even the slightest bulge. There wasn't one. In fact, she had never looked healthier. Her tan had lightened so that now only a slight glow remained.

Again she counted the days in her mind.

Yes, yes. It could be true. It had been just over six weeks since their wedding—and their wedding night. She smiled hopefully and crossed her fingers.

Before she could say anything to Jed, Caitlin knew she had to be absolutely sure. Going into the bedroom, she picked up the phone beside the bed. First she called Grace at the office, explaining that something had come up and she wouldn't be going into the office that day. She hung up and then made a second call, this time to Dr. Carter. Reaching his receptionist, she asked if she could make an appointment for that morning.

Skipping down the steps of the medical building, Caitlin wanted to shout the news to everyone she saw. *I'm pregnant! I'm going to have Jed's baby!*

She didn't, of course. But she did give the surprised parking lot attendant an extra-generous tip as she pulled up beside the gate house. She looked up at the boy, her eyes sparkling, and said, "Isn't it a beautiful day?"

Driving away, she realized that she hadn't exactly made sense. No wonder the boy had stared at her as if she were crazy—it wasn't beautiful at all. The sky was dark and overcast, promising rain before nightfall. Caitlin remembered the weather report she had heard that morning. The weatherman had said something about a string of storms heading up the coast from the Caribbean.

As she turned onto the road that led toward Ryan Acres, her mind began to wander. It would be winter soon, Caitlin thought. Next month was her birthday, then Thanksgiving. She had so much to be thankful for. Then came Christmas. She decided to buy presents for the baby. Just a few things for fun—a stuffed teddy bear or some tiny booties. Would it be a girl, she wondered, or a boy? When the doctor told her there were ways of finding out the sex of the baby, she said she didn't want to know. She didn't care, anyway. It would be nice to have a boy for Jed, Caitlin supposed. But then, Jed would probably tell her that he'd rather have a girl, a pretty little girl that he could spoil.

Caitlin pushed a cassette into the tape deck, and moments later Anita Baker's strong, bluesy voice came through the speakers. She tapped her fingers on the steering wheel in time to the music. *I've got to figure out how to tell Jed*, she thought as she drove.

By the time she turned into the long, oak-lined driveway at Ryan Acres, she decided she would tell him that night over a romantic dinner. Melanie was going to a concert in Georgetown with Howard, so they would have the house to themselves.

She would have Margaret set a table in the rear sitting room. Unfortunately, they would have to close the doors that opened onto the conservatory because of the stormy weather. The orchids were in full bloom, though, so she would have some cut and arranged as a simple centerpiece. *Perfect*, she thought. *White orchids with white candles. And the gold-rimmed Aynsley china, with a peach tablecloth.*

Suddenly she thought about the perfect way to break the news to Jed. The wine at dinner! She wasn't allowed to drink again until after the baby was born. So at dinner that night she would make sure there was a bottle of sparkling mineral water sitting in the wine bucket along with a bottle of burgundy for Jed. He would naturally be curious and ask why she wasn't having any wine. That was when she would tell him. She sighed happily, barely able to wait.

Hurrying into the house, Caitlin went upstairs to change her clothes. She knew she should spend a couple of hours working in the library, but she was just too excited to stare at reports and make business decisions. So instead, after putting on a pair of black leggings and an oversize yellow cotton sweater, she went down to the kitchen to talk to Mrs. Crowley about the menu for dinner.

"I'd like to have Jed's favorites tonight," she said. "Do we have any good steaks in the freezer?"

"Yes, ma'am," the cook replied. "We have those little filets mignons he likes so much."

"Oh, that's terrific," Caitlin said. "We'll have two of those, and two baked potatoes with sour cream, and a salad with that great honey-dill dressing. And for dessert"—she paused and bit her lip—"would it be too much trouble to bake a chocolate cake?"

"For you two?" The woman's plump face was beaming. "Of course it wouldn't be too much trouble. And I'll be sure to make the frosting nice and thick, too."

The sky had lightened and as she left the house to head down to the stable, Caitlin thought that it might not rain at all. In fact, it was almost too warm for the lightweight jacket she had put on over her sweater. Reaching the pasture rail, she paused to admire the newly finished track.

There was someone kneeling out there, apparently examining the dirt surface. Seeing the red hair, she figured it must be the new stable boy, Johnny Carns. Caitlin liked the kid, even admired him in ways. He worked hard, and he also seemed to love just being around the horses.

When he stood up, Caitlin raised her arm and waved to him. As he turned toward her, though, she realized it wasn't Johnny at all. True, the man was about the same height, and the color of his hair was the same carrot red. But he was older than Johnny. She noticed also that his face had the leathery look of a person who had spent a lot of time outside.

He's probably working on the new stable, she thought. She was about to nod politely and go find Jed, but just then an arm slipped around her waist. A bit startled, she looked up to see Jed smiling down at her.

"Hi, beautiful." He planted a quick kiss on her forehead. "Have you two met?" he asked, nodding toward the man from the track, who was now only about five feet from them.

"Oh—" She looked at the man again. "No, I'm afraid we haven't."

"Red, I'd like you to meet my wife, Caitlin Michaels. Caitlin, this is Red Meyers, our new jockey."

"Mrs. Michaels." The man nodded tersely. "It's a pleasure."

"Please, call me Caitlin. I'm so happy to finally

meet you, Mr. Meyers. I'm just sorry I wasn't here the other day when you first came to talk to my husband. But I must say, I was very impressed with your background and the horses you've ridden. I'm delighted that you've agreed to ride for Ryan Acres."

"Again, my pleasure, Mrs.—uh, Caitlin." He turned to Jed. "I was just checking out the new track. Very nice—very nice."

"Thank you," Jed replied. "Nothing but the best for Magic."

"Right—right," Red said. But he didn't really seem to be listening. His expression was preoccupied. "Well," he finally said, taking a step backward, "guess I'd better be going."

Jed and Caitlin watched as he walked away and got into the low, black sports car that was parked under a tree near the stable. As he drove away, Jed said, "Well, he's not exactly friendly, but Lou feels he's the best man for the job. And I guess that's what counts."

"Yes," Caitlin said as she put her arms around Jed's waist, already dismissing Red Meyers's slightly cool personality. "That's what counts."

Jed glanced at his watch. "Hey, aren't you back from the office a little early? I thought you had an appointment."

"Oh, I did, but it didn't last all that long," she

said easily. "So, I decided to come home and have lunch with you. And I thought as long as I was home I'd come down here and say 'hi' to Magic."

"I'm glad you did." Arm in arm, they walked slowly toward the barn. "Actually, I'm very glad you came home early," Jed said. "There's something I wanted to tell you."

"Really? What?" She glanced up at him.

"Well, when I was reading the paper this morning, I happened to spot an ad for a surfing competition. It's this Saturday, and I'm thinking of entering it. It should be a breeze compared to Hawaii."

"Wait—a surfing competition?" Caitlin felt as if she had been punched in the stomach. *No,* she thought, *it can't be.* How could there possibly be surfing anywhere near Ryan Acres? But she finally managed to ask, "Where is it?"

"In Virginia Beach," Jed replied. "It's only a few hours away. And since it's on a Saturday, when you don't have to go into the office, I thought you might like to come with me. We could even make a nice little trip of it. You know, go someplace nice for dinner afterward, stay over. There are some very nice hotels—"

"*No!*" Caitlin cried. She pulled away and turned to face him. "I won't go. Absolutely not.

And I don't want you to go, either." All she could think of was the monstrous, frightening waves she had seen in Hawaii. She had been absolutely terrified that Jed would get hurt, and she refused to go through that kind of fear again. Especially not now, not when Jed was going to be a father.

"Are we going to have the same argument we had in Hawaii?" Jed asked harshly. "Because if we are, I don't want to hear it. Surfing isn't any more dangerous than taking some horse over a high jump. But I've never asked you to stop riding, have I?"

"No, but—"

"But nothing." He shook his head impatiently. "I don't like it when you act this way, Caitlin. You were never demanding like this before we were married. Why are you doing it now?"

"I don't like surfing. It scares me," she responded lamely.

"Well, it doesn't scare me!" he said back. Then he calmed down slightly. "Look, I promise I'll be careful, okay?"

"But, Jed—" She almost told him about the baby. If he knew, she was sure he would agree not to do anything as dangerous as surfing.

"What?" he prompted, looking at her expectantly.

Her heart was in her throat. Here was her chance. Caitlin started to open her mouth, but then she realized she just couldn't do it. She couldn't use the news about the baby to win an argument. After looking at Jed for a long moment, she knew she was right. It was obvious that he wanted very much to take part in this competition. She was letting her fears get the best of her. Resolutely, Caitlin decided to postpone saying anything about the baby until after Saturday. It was already Thursday. What difference would a couple of days make? And then, once Jed knew, he would decide on his own to give up surfing. Yes, she told herself, this way was best for everyone.

"Nothing," she said with a weak smile. "I wasn't going to say anything." Reaching up, she ran a finger along the side of his jaw. "Go ahead and enter the competition. I love you, Jed, and I want you to do what you want to do. Just promise me you'll be careful."

"I promise. I'll be as careful as can be," he said, picking her up and swinging her around. As he set her down, he pulled her close. "Oh, Caitlin, I love you, too," he said in a low voice. "I love you more than anything in the world." He kissed her tenderly, and as the kiss ended, she leaned closer to him. She needed to feel the safety of being in his arms.

Stroking her silky black hair, he said, "I don't ever want to hurt you, Caitlin. Don't ever forget that."

"I won't, Jed," she promised. "I won't."

The storm the weatherman had predicted finally arrived in the middle of the night. The fierce wind tore through the trees and splattered the rain against the windows. Wide-awake, Caitlin lay in bed, her head against Jed's chest. He was fast asleep, but she couldn't help being frightened by the storm. Maybe it would continue, worsen even, and the surfing competition would be canceled. Caitlin could only hope. *Then I can tell him about the baby,* she thought. *And he'll be so happy that he won't even mind not getting a chance to surf.*

By Saturday, however, the worst of the storm had passed. Only a few ragged clouds were left. Jed whistled happily as they drove toward the beach town. As Caitlin stole a look at his handsome profile, she could only wish that the day would go by quickly.

When they reached the beach where the competition was being held, Caitlin stared out at the ocean. The same absolute terror washed over her that she had felt when she was standing on that faraway beach in Hawaii. Determined not to let her feelings show, she remained quiet and waited while Jed got out of the car. He then went over and signed in with the officials, who were working out of a van parked nearby.

A small crowd of surfers gathered around the van. She watched as Jed spoke to someone, then started back toward her. His expression was not happy.

"There's a possibility that they might have to cancel the competition," he reported as he slid into the driver's seat beside her. "It seems that the storm that went through here left some rough water behind. The wave action might be too unpredictable."

"Oh, that's too bad," Caitlin said, trying hard not to sound happy about the news.

"Well, nothing's sure yet," Jed said. "Some of the guys over there are trying to talk them into going ahead. I don't think it's that bad." He paused, looking out at the water. "Anyway, I just came back to let you know what's happening. I want to go back over and do whatever I can to get this thing going." He pushed down the door handle. "After all, this is probably my last chance to go surfing until spring."

"But wait—don't you think it's best to leave the decision to the experts?" she said.

"Will you stop worrying?" He patted her hand. "I told you I'd be careful, and I will."

As she watched him return to the group, however, Caitlin couldn't help worrying. Her fears became even worse when she realized that the van parked just beyond the officials was an ambulance. If surfing wasn't any more dangerous than riding, she thought, then why was it there? There were no paramedics waiting at horse shows!

Finally, after what seemed like hours, Jed came back to the car again. That time he looked happier.

"It's on," he told her.

Caitlin got out of the car while Jed changed to his red wet suit and untied his surfboard, which had been strapped to the top of the car. "Why don't you go over there and sit with the other spectators," he said, pointing as he zipped up the front of his suit. "You can see a lot better there than you can sitting here in the car." She nodded numbly. Jed locked the car and handed her the keys. "After all, I want my cheering section to be where I can see you."

Caitlin dutifully went over to sit with the other spectators. From her perch on the top of a low wall that separated the sand from a cement walk, she kept her gaze fastened on Jed's bright red figure. He was standing at the edge of the surf, waiting for things to get started. Like Jed, most of the contestants were dressed in wet suits because the water had already turned quite cold. There were a lot of black suits and a scattering of colored ones, but Jed's was the only red one.

"Which one's yours?" a girl who was sitting beside her asked amiably.

Caitlin nodded toward Jed. "My husband's the one in red."

"He's cute," the girl added. "I'll bet he's good, too."

"I guess so." Caitlin didn't really want to get into a conversation with anyone—she just wanted the day to be over. But she couldn't just ignore the girl, who was only trying to be nice. Turning, she asked politely, "Is someone you know in the contest?"

"Yeah, my dad." The girl shook her head. "Can you believe it? He thinks he's still in his twenties. But then, once a surfer, always a surfer, I guess. He's the bald guy in the blue wet suit."

"He looks pretty good," Caitlin replied, impressed.

"Wait till you see him on the board. Oh, hey," she said, pointing, "there goes your husband now."

Caitlin quickly turned to see Jed, lying flat on his board, paddling out through the incoming waves. With him were five other surfers. "How do you tell who wins?" she asked, suddenly feeling very stupid.

"They're judged on form. Those guys probably won't even start at the same time. What happens is, each person decides on the wave they think will be best, and they catch it." She pointed again. "Look, there's my dad." Caitlin saw that the older man was just starting to ride a wave. As she watched, he stood up, then maneuvered the board so that he was riding the wave high on its side. "It's how you handle yourself, your style, that's important."

"Oh, I understand." Caitlin nodded. Suddenly she really wanted to see Jed perform well. Maybe she had been all wrong about surfing. After all, if this girl's father could do it without getting hurt, surely Jed could do it. He'd always been a good athlete.

"Look, excuse me," the girl said, interrupting Caitlin's thoughts. "I want to go down and congratulate my dad." She shrugged. "A little encouragement never hurts, right?"

"Right." Caitlin nodded and gave a friendly wave. The girl walked across the sand toward the water.

And that's exactly what she was going to do, too, she told herself, encourage Jed. Leaning forward, she looked for Jed's bright red wet suit among the other surfers. Oh, there he was. Standing up to get a better view, she saw him catch the swell of a wave. She watched the wave build, then begin to break in a long line of white foam. Jed was right on top of it. Nearby, someone said, "Hey, check out that guy in red! Good, isn't he?"

He is! she thought with pride. She wanted to turn and tell the person who had spoken that the guy in red was her husband, but just then someone standing beside her gasped loudly. Seconds later, she realized it was for Jed. He was down, gone. Right in front of her eyes, he had been sucked under by a giant wave.

"Jed, no! Jed!" she screamed wildly. Tears sprang to her eyes.

"What happened?" someone asked. "Where's that guy in red?"

"He wiped out."

"I know, but where is he?"

"I don't know," his friend answered. "I can't see him. Can you?"

"Oh, man, he's gone."

"I'm going to get the paramedics. He's going to need them when he comes up."

"If he does. That wave was a real killer."

Killer—killer—killer. The words played over and over in Caitlin's mind as she searched the blue-green water, looking for any sign of Jed. *Oh, please,* she screamed silently. *He can't be gone. Oh, please, God, no!*

8

"There he is!" a woman in the crowd screamed.

Her heart suddenly pounding with hope, Caitlin turned to see where the woman was looking. Her hope was dashed by the terrible sight that met her gaze. Jed was lying crumpled at the edge of the water, his body partially covered by the foamy surf.

He wasn't moving—not a bit.

Caitlin wanted to go to him, but she couldn't. She couldn't seem to move. She was frozen by her fear.

Then, all at once, the crowd surged forward, rushing toward him. Caitlin saw the paramedics run awkwardly through the sand, weighted down with their lifesaving equipment. Still she couldn't move. She was afraid of what she would find, afraid that Jed was *dead*.

The paramedics loaded Jed carefully onto a stretcher. Then they put some kind of a supportive device around his shoulders and neck.

He's alive, she realized. Relief flooded through her.

The thought enabled her to move and she moved forward, started running toward the men who were carrying Jed. She reached them just as they came to the low wall. She tried to get close enough to see him, but was pushed aside.

"Please don't get in our way, miss," a paramedic told her. "This man is badly injured, and we have to get him to the hospital immediately."

"He's my husband," she cried out, reaching past the man to touch Jed.

"Caitlin?" Jed called in a weak voice.

"Jed. Jed, darling, I'm here," Caitlin sobbed.

"Did you say he's your husband?" the paramedic who'd spoken before asked her as the rear doors of the ambulance were thrown open.

"Yes, he is," she said.

"You want to come along with us then? If you'd rather you can take your own car, or have someone bring you to the hospital. You will be needed there to sign the admittance papers, though, so you'd better hurry."

"I want to come with you, of course," Caitlin replied, concerned only about being near Jed.

"Come on, then," he told her. With a quick movement, he helped her up and into a small seat close to Jed. Jumping in, he went right to Jed's side as the doors were slammed shut from outside.

Moments later they were speeding away, toward the hospital. Caitlin could hear the siren, but the noise was muffled. There were other sounds, too—Jed's labored breathing, the *wooosh-wooosh* of the blood-pressure cuff as the paramedic inflated it, the squawk of the radio as another paramedic called in to report that they were on their way. She glanced at Jed, her heart in her throat. Oddly, he didn't look badly hurt. His face was a bit pale, but that was all. They had cut open the sleeves of Jed's wet suit in order to get to his arms. One of the paramedics inserted an intravenous needle in the arm without the blood pressure cuff. A bag of clear liquid was attached by a tube and she could see the liquid dripping slowly into the tube and running down into Jed's arm.

Oh, God, please let him be all right, she pleaded silently.

Caitlin wanted to ask the paramedic how Jed was doing, but she didn't. She didn't think she could bear it if the man gave her bad news. And beyond that, she didn't want to distract him. Jed needed all of his attention right then.

At last they pulled up to the hospital emergency room. Caitlin stood, feeling absolutely helpless, as they wheeled Jed into the emergency room and then into a smaller examining room. When she tried to follow, a doctor told her firmly that she had to wait outside.

Feeling utterly alone, she walked over to a row of molded plastic chairs lined against one side of the long hall. She sat down, wondering what she should do next. *There must be something*, she thought frantically.

People bustled in and out of the room where they had taken Jed. Caitlin couldn't tell whether they were doctors or technicians, but the commotion upset her. If Jed needed so many people to take care of him, the news couldn't be good.

Soon a woman in a light blue uniform, carrying a clipboard and some forms, came over and sat beside her. The woman pushed the clipboard toward Caitlin.

"I'm sorry to bother you, Mrs. Michaels, but I must ask you to fill out these forms so that your husband can be properly admitted."

Caitlin took the pen the woman handed her, but as she looked down at the printed sheet of paper, nothing seemed to make sense. She forced herself to focus on the top line. "Michaels, Jed," she printed where it asked for the patient's name.

"Oh, and I'll need you to complete these insurance forms as well," the woman said.

Caitlin stared at her, shocked at the amount of paperwork.

"I'm sorry," the woman said apologetically. "But it's absolutely necessary. Otherwise we can't admit him."

"Yes, of course." Caitlin swallowed hard, forcing back her tears. She wanted to take the forms the woman had shoved at her, tear them up, and throw them right back in her face. "I'll fill them out, really. But could you please—leave me alone right now?"

The woman stood up. "When you've finished, just bring them to the nurses' station," she said and left.

Caitlin stared at the forms, concentrating on filling in the right information. She completed two lines, then looked up again, distracted. Across the hall, she saw a pay phone. *Melanie.* She should call Melanie. But somehow she just couldn't, not until she had some good news. Not until she knew Jed was going to be all right.

And he will be all right, she told herself fiercely, bending over the clipboard again.

Inside the examining room, Jed regained consciousness. The preliminary tests had just been completed, and the doctor was standing beside him. A cut on Jed's right leg had been stitched, and now there was a neat white bandage over it.

"I—I can't feel my legs," Jed said in a faint voice. He looked around the room wildly, panic in his eyes. "What's wrong with my legs? Doctor?"

"Yes, Mr. Michaels, I'm right here." The doctor hesitated, then wiped his hand over his mouth. "I'm not the kind of doctor who likes to beat around the bush," he sighed heavily. "I believe in telling my patients—"

"What is it, doctor? What's wrong with me?"

"You're paralyzed from the shoulders down. We don't know why, or for how long. Until the X rays are processed, we won't know anything for sure. I'm sorry," he added, his eyes kind and gentle.

"I'm—I'm paralyzed?" Jed stared at the man in disbelief.

"I'm sorry, Mr. Michaels." The doctor shook his head. "I really am sorry."

The doctor stepped out of the examining room and closed the door quietly behind him. He looked down the hallway and saw Caitlin. She jumped up as he came toward her.

"Mrs. Michaels?" He smiled softly and held out his hand. "Hi, I'm Dr. Miles."

She nodded impatiently. "How is he? How is Jed?"

"Let's sit down over here, shall we?" Dr. Miles took her arm and led her into a nearby lounge.

Numbly, Caitlin allowed the doctor to guide her. Then, just as numbly, she listened as he told her Jed was paralyzed. Caitlin burst into tears.

The doctor waited a moment, then told her that Jed's chances for a *full* recovery were slim. "I'm so sorry, Mrs. Michaels. I wish I had better news." He reached into his pocket and handed her a handkerchief.

"But it is good news," Caitlin said through her tears. She took the handkerchief and blotted her eyes. "All that matters is that he's alive. Jed's alive." She smiled for the first time that day. "When can I see him?"

"Soon," Dr. Miles told her gently. "But I think it would be best to let him get settled into his room first." He nodded, as if to himself. "He's been told he's paralyzed, and it's not going to be easy for him to accept. Give him some time. You might even want to go to the coffee shop, have something to eat or a drink." He glanced down at his watch. "It's been awhile since your husband was brought in. You must be hungry. Some food would do you good."

"No, really," Caitlin said. "I just want to see Jed."

"I don't think that's a good idea," he said, patting her shoulder. "You both should have some time alone right now."

"All right," Caitlin replied irritably. Forcing herself to stay in control, she asked. "What time shall I come back?"

The doctor checked his watch again. "Give him a couple of hours, maybe until about seven. He'll be on the eighth floor. You can check at the nurses' station; they'll tell you which room."

As soon as the doctor started down the hall, Caitlin went to the phone. She called Melanie first, explaining what had happened as gently as she could. Melanie, of course, wanted to join Caitlin right away. But Caitlin managed to convince her that she wouldn't be allowed to visit Jed, anyway.

"Maybe they'll let you see him tomorrow," she told her. "In fact, I'm sure they will." She could hear Jed's sister sobbing softly. "Melanie, don't cry, please. Jed's alive, and that's the important thing." She stopped, thinking for a moment. "We have to think positively. I'll be home later

108

tonight, and we can talk about what's best for Jed then. Then you can drive back down here with me in the morning."

They spoke for a few moments longer, then Caitlin hung up. Immediately, she placed another call. This one was to her father, Dr. Gordon Westlake. *He'll know what to do,* she thought. He'd tell her everything was going to be all right, and then he'd find someone who could help Jed.

The phone seemed to ring forever before her father answered. At the sound of her troubled voice, he apologized quickly, saying he had just come in the door. "What is it, honey? What's wrong?"

Caitlin couldn't help herself. At the sound of her father's comforting voice, she started crying again. Between sobs, she told him about the accident, and what the doctor had said about Jed's condition. She drew in a ragged breath, then pleaded, "Can you do something—find some treatment or something? There has to be a way to help Jed. There has to be!"

"Try not to worry too much, honey. We'll figure something out." Dr. Westlake spoke to Caitlin for a few more minutes, then he said, "Look, sweetheart, I'm going to make some calls, okay? I'll see what I can come up with."

Hanging up, Caitlin was about to do as Dr. Miles had suggested and go down to the coffee shop to wait out the next couple of hours. She turned away from the phone and started down the corridor. But then she stopped, thought for a moment, and went back over to the phone. She picked up the receiver and placed a call to Los Angeles. "Yes, may I please have the number of a Mrs. Katherine Michaels?"

9

After speaking to the doctors once again, Caitlin poked her head around the door to Jed's room. His eyes were closed, and she wasn't sure if he was asleep, or not.

"Jed?" she called softly.

There was no answer.

Almost on tiptoe, she crossed the room to stand beside the high hospital bed. The rails were up. Jed's arms were lying on top of the light blanket that was tucked neatly around his body. Instantly, she felt a sob rise in her throat. Jed never slept that way. His side of the bed was usually a tangle of covers as he sprawled on his stomach, then restlessly rolled over onto his back.

She choked back the sob, then in what she

hoped was a normal-sounding voice she said, "Jed? Are you awake?"

He opened his eyes. But he didn't look in her direction. Instead, he stared straight up at the ceiling.

"Hi, darling, it's me—Caitlin."

She waited, but he didn't say anything. Suddenly she was afraid that there was something wrong, that he couldn't speak, or that maybe he wasn't able to hear her.

"*Jed?*" she cried in alarm. She took a step closer, her hand on the bed rails.

He finally moved, turning his head away from her. "Go away, Caitlin." His voice was low, but she heard the words distinctly.

"What? No, I won't—"

"Yes," he said, still not looking at her. "I don't want to see you. Please, just go away."

"You don't mean that. I love you, Jed, that's all that matters. Please—please look at me."

"Go *away!*"

Caitlin didn't know what to say or do. She just continued to stand there, hoping he would turn his head and look at her.

Finally, with a terrible fear settling into her stomach, she turned away and quietly left the room.

* * *

Jed heard the door close as Caitlin left. The room seemed so empty and cold without her. He turned his head and looked at the door, wanting desperately to jump up and run after her. He wanted to grab her, hold her in his arms, and tell her how much he loved her. But he couldn't. He would never be able to do those things again. And that was why he had to give her her freedom—no matter how it hurt him then.

He thought about what the doctor had told him, and it hadn't taken him long to realize that he would never move again. He knew what he had to do. Caitlin was young and strong—he wasn't about to ask her to care for a husband who was absolutely helpless. He was no good to her now. Why? he thought bitterly. Why hadn't the surf just finished him? He wished that he had been killed, that Caitlin would be able to remember him as he had been, as a whole person. Maybe—maybe if he willed it hard enough, he could close his eyes and just slip away. But instead of closing his eyes, he continued to stare up at the ceiling, hoping for a miracle.

Caitlin still had Jed's car keys, which he had given to her earlier in the day. Taking a cab, she went back to the beach to pick up the car.

Even though it was dark, she saw the moment she got there that someone had found Jed's surfboard and left it next to the car. She looked at the board with loathing. Picking it up, she angrily heaved it away into the sand. Then she got into the car, backed up, and sped away from the place she knew she would never forget.

When she got back to Ryan Acres, it was well after midnight. Melanie was waiting for her in the library with Howard. As she walked into the room, she noticed that Howard was holding one of Melanie's slender hands in his, gripping it tightly. Caitlin was glad Melanie had someone like Howard to lean on, but looking at the two of them together made her feel even more alone.

Melanie jumped up from the couch as Caitlin entered the room. "How is he? Is he any better? Did you talk to the doctor after you called me? Did you get to see Jed?"

Caitlin was so tired, she didn't know which question to answer first.

Realizing she was exhausted, Howard poured a small amount of brandy into a glass. He handed it to Caitlin, who had collapsed into a chair. "Here. You look as though you could use this."

Gratefully, Caitlin accepted the glass. As she took a sip of the strong liquor, she could feel herself beginning to relax. Then she remembered the baby and set the glass aside. Taking a deep breath, she told Melanie and Howard as much as she knew.

"I called my father, and he's going to see what he can do. So, we have to keep hoping," she explained. "I'm going back down there early tomorrow morning. Would you like to go with me, Melanie?" In the back of her mind, she was hoping that Jed's sister could convince him to see her. "I'd like to get there first thing in the morning."

"Of course I want to go with you," Melanie replied. She shook her head. "Can't we bring Jed back here? I mean, there's a great hospital in Middletown. If he was there, we could be close to him."

"I already thought of that. Actually I wanted to have him taken to Meadow Valley, my dad's hospital. But the doctors have all agreed that he can't be moved yet."

"Is there anything I can do?" Howard asked gently.

"Thank you, but I can't think of anything at the moment," Caitlin replied. "Tomorrow's Sunday, and although I hate disturbing my employees on the weekend, I think I'm going to call my secretary, Grace, as well as Randolph Woods.

I don't want to have to deal with Ryan Mining business for the next several days. Unless there's a real emergency, of course. But Grace and Randolph can take care of everything else."

"Woods is a good man," Howard said, agreeing. "I'm sure he'll be able to handle the day-to-day business."

"Yes." Caitlin nodded. Running a hand through her tangled black hair, she said wearily, "I'll see you in the morning, okay? I'm going to try to get some sleep." Going over to Melanie, she took her hands and gave them a squeeze. In a low voice, she said, "Don't worry, Melanie. We're going to find a way to beat this. Somehow, we're going to help Jed get better." Then she put her hand on Howard's shoulder. "Thank you, Howard—for being here." Forcing herself to smile, she turned and left the room.

Upstairs in her bedroom, she turned on the light and looked around the spacious and beautifully decorated room. She felt a terrible, desperate loneliness. Skipping her usual nighttime routine, she undressed quickly. But just as she was about to put on her nightgown, she dropped it back into the drawer instead. Going into Jed's dressing room, she searched for and found his favorite pajamas. She held the top of

116

the soft cotton garment to her face and inhaled. It smelled like Jed.

She slipped the pajama top on, then went back into the bedroom and crawled under the covers on Jed's side of the huge bed. Closing her eyes, she wrapped her arms around herself. Her last thoughts as she fell asleep were that she wasn't alone. Part of Jed—the baby—was with her. *The baby.* The wonderful, happy surprise she had wanted to tell him about. She couldn't say anything now. The baby would have to stay her secret for a while longer.

Making the long drive back to Virginia Beach the next morning, Caitlin and Melanie were silent for most of the trip, each lost in her own thoughts. Caitlin was hoping that Jed would see and talk to Melanie. Maybe after that, he would be ready to talk to her.

But Jed refused to speak to anyone. Not long after she went in, Melanie came out of Jed's room, tears spilling down her cheeks. "Caitlin, he's just lying there. He won't even look at me."

Caitlin's heart sank, but she tried not to let it show. Putting her arm around her shoulders, she said, "We just have to give him more time, Melanie. He'll change his mind. I know he will." *Time*, Caitlin repeated to herself. *The doctor said it would take time. But how long?* she wondered. How long could she go on like this?

The next day she went back to the hospital alone, arriving just in time for morning visiting hours. Going into Jed's room, she called to him and then stood there for several long minutes. She could tell he was pretending to be asleep. Finally she left.

Deciding to wait several hours before trying to see him again, she went for a walk. She strolled around the busy resort town for a while, not really seeing what was going on around her. Back at the hospital, Caitlin stopped at the gift shop in the lobby and bought some flowers to take to Jed. If he wouldn't see her, she could at least make it hard for him to forget she had been there.

Getting off the elevator at the eighth floor, she was passing the nurses' station on her way to Jed's room. A young woman in a white uniform saw her and called out to her.

"Excuse me, Mrs. Michaels? There's someone to see you in the waiting room. She says she's your mother-in-law."

Jed's mother! Caitlin's mind was racing. Jed's mother was there, in Virginia. She remembered their stumbling phone conversation as she had hastily explained what had happened. Caitlin had felt awkward and nervous as she suggested to Jed's mother that she might want to come to see her son. But from the other woman's cool response, Caitlin hadn't thought she would.

"Thank you," she told the nurse, then headed toward the waiting room.

Caitlin wasn't sure what sort of person she expected to find as she walked into the small room just to the right of the nurses' station. Jed's mother had lived in the Los Angeles area for several years. Would she look very chic? Or maybe she was the type who wore miniskirts and tried to look too young? Caitlin wasn't prepared for the slender, attractive woman who rose when she entered the room.

"You must be Caitlin," the woman said, coming toward her, her hand outstretched. "I've seen your photo many times in the newspapers."

"Hello, Mrs. Michaels." Caitlin assessed the woman. She had to be close to fifty, but she looked much younger. Her skin had a healthy glow and her dark hair was attractively cut. She wore only the slightest bit of makeup, and she was dressed conservatively in a beige silk dress.

"Oh, my dear, I'm so glad to finally meet you," she said, clasping Caitlin's hand. "And, please, call me Kathy. Everyone does." She shook her head. "It's so hard to believe—my daughter-in-law." With a faint smile, she said, "The last time I saw Jed, he was so young. And now he's married. . . ." Her voice trailed off. Then she said, "How badly is he hurt? I wanted to talk to the doctor myself, but they said he isn't here."

"Well—Jed is in pretty bad shape," she said, not knowing what else to say. "As I told you on the phone, he's paralyzed, but he's going to get better. I know he is."

"Caitlin, he won't see me." The older woman's voice seemed to catch in her throat. "I've come all this way, and he won't even see me."

"He refuses to see me, too," Caitlin told her softly. Putting her arm around her mother-in-law's shoulders, she led her to a chair. As they both sat down, Caitlin suddenly felt very sorry for this woman. It was obvious that Mrs. Michaels wanted to make up for all the time she had not been there for Jed. For Melanie, too. But would either of her children let her back into their lives? It was impossible to tell. "I think you have to give Jed time—to get used to you again, as well as to the paralysis." She knew it was the right thing to say, but Caitlin hated how hollow her words sounded. Was that what they were all

supposed to do, get used to Jed's paralysis?
Accept it? She knew she couldn't—not now, not
ever!

"Yes, yes, of course. He's got every right to be
very angry with me." Mrs. Michaels pulled a
handkerchief out of her purse and dabbed at her
eyes. "It's just that after all these years, I wanted
to make up for leaving them." She looked at
Caitlin. "When you called, I was shocked at first.
But then I began thinking. I was so selfish,
leaving my children the way I did. And to run
away with a man I'd just met, too. I wanted to
take them with me, but I couldn't. They had
everything there on the ranch. What could I
have given them?" She closed her eyes and
swallowed a sob. "But I never stopped thinking
of them, not for a single day. Your love for your
children never ends." Opening her eyes, she put
her hand over Caitlin's. "You'll find that out
when you have children of your own."

Yes, Caitlin thought. *I think I already know.* With
a smile, she looked at Mrs. Michaels directly.
"Why don't you come back to Ryan Acres with
me." Melanie was there, Caitlin thought. And if
Melanie and her mother could accept each other,
then, together, they might be able to help Jed.
"You must be exhausted from your flight. Come

121

with me, and we'll both get some rest. Then we can come back again tomorrow—together."

It was late afternoon by the time Caitlin got back to Ryan Acres with Jed's mother. The drive from the hospital had been long, but they had talked the whole way. To her surprise, Caitlin found that she really liked Mrs. Michaels. It was hard not to like her. She was honest about the mistakes she had made, and she did want a chance to make up for them.

Caitlin was so sure that Mrs. Michaels had changed that when they came through the front door, she was almost taken aback by Melanie's violent reaction.

At first, Melanie stared at her mother, her expression a mixture of shock and disbelief. Finally she said, "Mother, is that really you?"

"Yes—yes, it is, darling," Mrs. Michaels replied hesitantly. Then she took a step toward Melanie. "I had to come—to see Jed." She smiled weakly. "And, of course, I wanted to see you."

"Well, I *don't* want to see you!" Melanie retorted hotly. She stepped back, away from her mother. "And I certainly don't see any reason for you to be here." She shot an accusatory glance at Caitlin. "I can't believe you let her come here after what she did!"

"At least hear her out. Let her tell you her side," Caitlin suggested softly. "After all, she is your mother. Don't you think she deserves a chance to explain?"

"As far as I'm concerned," Melanie replied evenly, "she gave up that privilege a long, long time ago." Turning away, she added, "This is your house, Caitlin, and you have a right to invite whomever you want to stay here. But don't expect me to welcome her with open arms, because I won't—ever!"

Melanie started to leave, then stopped and turned back. "Oh, your father's here. He's in the library. I—I think he has some news about Jed's condition, but he wouldn't tell me. He said he'd rather talk to you first."

Caitlin's heart was in her throat. Could it be good news? Maybe her father had found someone who could help Jed. But then, what if it was bad news? "Thank you," she finally told Melanie. "I'll go see what he wants."

Melanie nodded and ran up the stairs without looking back. Turning to face Jed's mother, Caitlin said, "Please, I hope you'll forgive me for being so rude, but I want to speak to my father alone first. Then I will introduce you two."

"Of course," Mrs. Michaels said. "Take your time."

Ringing for Rollins, Caitlin asked him to show Mrs. Michaels into the living room and bring her some tea. Then she excused herself.

Entering the library, Caitlin found her father standing by the window, his back to her. "Have you found anything out?" she asked. "Is it good news?"

"I don't know yet," Dr. Westlake said, turning around. They both sat down on the couch. Taking her hands in his, he said, "I've spoken with a doctor I know, in Boston. He says there's a doctor at Harvard Medical who's been doing research on spinal injuries. He's experimenting with an operation that sounds very promising."

"Really? Oh, do you think he'd see Jed?"

"I don't know. A lot depends on exactly what kind of operation this is and what kind of injury Jed has sustained." Dr. Westlake looked at Caitlin and said, "Honey, I don't want you to get too excited about this. Not until I've had a chance to talk to this guy."

"When will that be?"

"I don't know. I put a call in to him this morning, but he hasn't called back yet. I'll keep trying, though."

"Thank you so much," Caitlin said, leaning over to hug her father. "I appreciate everything you've done, I really do."

"I know you do. And don't worry, we'll find a way to help Jed." He kissed her forehead and smoothed back a strand of hair. "I promise."

Caitlin looked up at her father and smiled. Then she gasped. "Oh, no. I almost forgot about Jed's mother. She's in the living room."

After she introduced her father to Jed's mother, Caitlin turned to Dr. Westlake. "Why don't you stay and have some tea with us? I'll have Margaret bring in some more hot water."

"Actually, that would be very nice," Dr. Westlake replied, sitting down on one of the chairs across from Mrs. Michaels. "It's been a long day."

Caitlin rang for the maid, but before fresh tea could be brought, Rollins appeared in the doorway.

"Excuse me, ma'am, but there's a call for you. It's your secretary calling back."

"Oh, thank you, Rollins." She turned to her father and Jed's mother. "I'm sorry. I'll be right back."

As she left the room, Caitlin noticed that there seemed to be a rapport between the two. They were lost in conversation by the time she stepped into the hall.

* * *

"Jed's a fine young man," Dr. Westlake said. "I couldn't ask for anyone better for my daughter."

"I'm glad you think so," Mrs. Michaels replied, setting down her cup. "You know, I envy you. You and Caitlin seem so close. I love my son, and yet I don't know him. In my mind, I still think of him as a boy." She shook her head. "But of course, he's not."

"I think I know how you must feel," Dr. Westlake said.

"Oh?"

Dr. Westlake paused as the maid brought in the fresh tea, set a cup down in front of him and filled it. When she left, he tried to explain. "I'm not sure how much you know about my situation, but I didn't even know I had a daughter until Caitlin was sixteen."

"I've heard some of the story," Mrs. Michaels replied in a low, polite tone. "A lot has been written about Caitlin since she took over Ryan Mining, and—well, you can understand my interest."

"Of course." Dr. Westlake paused, then went on. "Anyway, we were reunited, and I've tried very hard to make up for all that lost time."

"Have you succeeded?"

"I think so. Caitlin and I are very close, closer than many parents and children." Suddenly he realized what he had said. "I'm so sorry. That was thoughtless of me."

"No, don't apologize." Jed's mother smiled thoughtfully. "I really wanted to know. I just hope that I can do the same."

The phone call from her secretary took longer than she had expected. When Caitlin finally returned to the living room, there was no one there. Her father and Mrs. Michaels had disappeared. She was wondering where they might have gone when Rollins appeared in the doorway.

"Your father asked me to tell you that he and Mrs. Michaels went for a walk."

"Oh, thank you, Rollins."

Good, Caitlin thought. *At least someone else likes Jed's mother.* "I didn't have a chance to tell you before, Rollins, but Mrs. Michaels will be staying for a few days. Would you please take her bag upstairs to the blue guest room, and have Margaret make sure the bed is made up."

"Very good, ma'am." Rollins nodded.

As he turned to leave, Margaret came into the room. "Excuse me, ma'am, there's another phone call for you."

Caitlin sighed. "All right. I'll take it in the library."

As she left the room, her thoughts were bouncing around wildly inside her head. Had Jed taken a turn for the worse? Was the hospital calling her for permission to operate? Or maybe—no, she refused to think about it.

"Hello," she said in a nervous, fearful voice. When she heard the familiar voice on the other end of the line, she wanted to cry with relief. It was Jed.

"Caitlin—" His voice was weak, but at least he was calling her. That must mean he was better, she reasoned.

"It's really you! Oh, Jed—" She paused, blinking back her tears. "How are you feeling? Tell me everything."

"I want to see you, Caitlin," he said flatly.

"I'll come right away. I'll be there—"

"You can't," he said, interrupting. "Visiting hours are over for today. Come in the morning, okay?"

"I'm sure they'd let me see you now. I am your wife, after all." She stopped. "Jed?" There was no answer. They had been disconnected.

She quickly called the hospital back and asked for Jed's room, explaining that she had been talking to him and they had been cut off.

"One moment, please," the operator said. There was silence as Caitlin was put on hold.

Then, a moment later, the woman came back on. "I'm sorry, ma'am. Mr. Michaels is no longer taking calls. He's had his phone shut off for the evening."

"But—I was just speaking to him," Caitlin explained. "I'm his wife. Surely if you just check again—"

"I really am very sorry," the operator replied. "Mr. Michaels was quite insistent that he not be disturbed."

"Oh, well, that's all right," she told the operator. "I understand. Good night."

Shaking her head, she hung up. Why wouldn't Jed talk to her? she wondered. Caitlin shrugged. It didn't really matter. What mattered was that Jed wanted to see her!

10

Caitlin was bursting with happiness as she headed toward Virginia Beach the next morning. Even the weather seemed to be cooperating.

Not a trace of the weekend storm was left, and the sky was clear and pure. It was the kind of blue sky that made the rest of the landscape seem dazzlingly bright. The rolling hills that flashed by seemed especially green, and the yellow and red autumn leaves popped out at Caitlin in bursts of color.

Yes, she thought, putting a Huey Lewis tape in the deck and turning up the volume, the last few days had been a dreadful trial for everyone. But Caitlin was sure now that everything was going to be all right.

Jed wanted to see her!

He loved her and she loved him. Together they would face whatever problems lay ahead. As long as they had each other, they could face anything.

Caitlin even felt hopeful about Jed's relationship with his mother. The older woman had confided in Caitlin the evening before that she and Dr. Westlake had talked for a long time about their children—and their mistakes.

"Your father convinced me not to give up hope," she said as they sipped their coffee. "He said that you hated him for a short time after you first discovered that he was your father." She looked at Caitlin shyly. "Oh, I know the situations are quite different. He didn't abandon you and your mother, while I did leave my husband and children. But your father still had to earn your trust and love, which is what I've got to do with Jed and Melanie. Somehow, I've got to make up for my mistakes." She smiled. "Your father said that now that they're adults, Jed and Melanie should be able to at least *understand* what I did throwing away everything for love."

Yes, Caitlin thought, *they should.* Perhaps if she explained to Jed how his mother felt, he would understand and forgive her. And then maybe Melanie would, too. Caitlin truly hoped so.

131

* * *

Caitlin was smiling as she walked into Jed's room, carrying a cheerful bouquet of yellow mums. Setting the flowers down on the dresser, she turned to Jed.

"Hi ya'," she said softly, as she walked over to the side of his bed. "How are you feeling? Can I get you anything?" She bent down and gently kissed his forehead. "I've been so happy since you called. I could hardly sleep last night." She laughed. "Finally I just got up. I got dressed and went down to see Magic. He sends his love—at least, I think he does. When I left his stall, he—"

"Caitlin!" Jed burst out angrily. "Stop it! Just stop it!"

"I'm sorry." Caitlin apologized quickly, taken aback by Jed's harsh words. "How thoughtless of me to babble on like that. I'll just sit down, and we can talk about whatever you want."

She started to pull the chair up so she could sit down beside the bed.

"Don't," Jed said, interrupting. "You're not going to be staying long."

"Of course I am." Caitlin argued automatically. But looking into Jed's eyes, she felt a wave of panic rising inside her. The expression in his eyes was hard and cold as steel. He had never

132

looked at her that way before. Lamely, she said, "The nurse said I could visit for twenty minutes."

"You're not staying because I don't want you to stay," Jed said clearly. "The only reason I asked you to come here was to tell you something. After that, I don't ever want to see you again."

"Jed, this is crazy. You're not making sense. Please, tell me you don't mean that."

"I do," he said assuring her. "Caitlin, I want an annulment. I don't want us to be married anymore."

"What?" She stared at him, stunned. She couldn't have heard him right. "You want a what?"

"Caitlin, please, listen to me. I'm tired and I don't want to argue with you."

Caitlin shook her head. She was gripping the bed rail so hard that her knuckles had turned white.

"Yes. I've had plenty of time to think about what I've become. I hate what I am, Caitlin, and if we stayed together, I'd hate you, too. I'd hate you for being healthy and whole, for reminding me of the things I can't do anymore. And what about you, Caitlin? I won't let you waste your life married to an invalid."

133

"It won't be a waste!" she cried. "I love you, Jed. We *can* make a life together—a wonderful life."

"No! I've made up my mind," he said firmly. "I've already talked to a lawyer. Please, accept my decision—just as I've accepted my new life."

No! she wanted to cry out. She wanted to scream at him, to convince him that he was wrong. But his expression was so grim that it chilled Caitlin into silence. She backed away from the bed.

"Yes. Go away, Caitlin. Go!" With an exhausted sigh, he closed his eyes and turned away from her. "Just leave me alone. Please."

When Caitlin left, Jed opened his eyes again. Turning, he saw the yellow flowers she had brought him and winced. He would have the nurse get rid of them, give them to another patient. Maybe he would save just one. But, no, he couldn't. It was better if he didn't have any reminders of her. That way it would be easier to forget her.

Never, Jed thought. How could he forget her when he loved her more than life? Her beautiful face, her teasing laugh, her tender kisses—how could he forget those? Jed knew he couldn't. He'd always love Caitlin—forever. No matter what.

* * *

Caitlin stood outside Jed's door. Hot tears burned in her eyes, but she blinked them back. She couldn't cry now. Not when she needed to be strong. She wasn't going to let Jed give up, and neither would she. Somehow, she would find a way. . . .

After Jed's accident, Caitlin had gone to see Jeff at the stable, asking him to take over as temporary manager.

"I'll happily do whatever I can," he had told her. "But you must realize that I don't know much about horseracing. I can certainly take care of the other horses, but I'm not so sure about Magic Man."

"That's all right," she said assuringly. "You just keep everything else running smoothly. Johnny will take care of Magic, and Lou Becker will be here every day to see to his training. I need you to oversee everything else, to keep things running smoothly." She had had to force a convincing smile. "While he's recovering, I'm sure Jed will appreciate knowing you're handling things."

Jeff agreed, and thinking everything would run smoothly Caitlin had turned her thoughts to helping Jed.

135

Johnny Carns, meanwhile, was becoming more and more devoted to Magic Man. He admired the way Lou Becker was training him, too. They had a surefire winner. "If he would just get rid of Red Meyers, that is." Johnny had been doing a little checking up on the jockey, and he didn't like what he'd found. He'd gone over to the stable where he worked before coming to Ryan Acres, and talked to some of the guys there. Not one of them liked Red. And even worse, none of them respected him, either.

"I know for a fact that Red Meyers is trouble," a stable boy in his late forties told Johnny as they sat in the sun on bales of hay. "He's thrown a couple of races that I know of. Of course, nothing's ever been proven." The man took a long drag on his cigarette and winked broadly. "You know how those things can be covered up—if there's enough money involved." Johnny nodded. "Now forget what I said."

Returning to Ryan Acres, Johnny was more determined than ever to get rid of Red. But he needed proof before he could go to the Michaelses. Four days after Jed's accident, he got it. He was coming out of the tack room when he saw Red.

The jockey was standing just outside Jed's office. After looking both ways, he opened the door and went inside. Since the tack room was located behind the office, Johnny was certain that Red hadn't seen him. He crossed the hall and stood to one side of the partially open door. He waited for a moment. Then he heard Red speaking on the phone.

So that's what he was doing in there, Johnny thought to himself. But there was nothing wrong with using the phone. Why, then, had he been sneaking around that way? He must not want anyone to overhear his phone call, Johnny reasoned. Leaning as close to the door as he dared, he tried to hear what Red was saying.

"Good, all right. . . . Hard to keep him from winning, though." Then there was a long pause. "Five grand won't cut it. It's ten or no deal." Red paused again, obviously listening to what the other person was saying. "Okay, you've got a deal, Mr.—" Suddenly Red stopped speaking. Johnny heard the phone being put down and footsteps start across the room.

Thinking fast, he grabbed a water bucket that was sitting nearby. As Red opened the door and looked out, Johnny walked by looking as if he was on his way to do something. Red closed the

137

door again and went back to the phone. *Whew! What a close call!* the boy thought as he continued down the hall.

Picking up the receiver, Red said, "It's okay. I thought I heard someone, but it was just that kid who takes care of the horse."

The man on the other end must have said, "Get rid of him."

"Okay, I'll talk to Becker about him. I don't think there's any real problem, but it's better to be safe."

Later that afternoon, while Johnny was grooming Magic, Lou Becker came up to him. "You're doing an excellent job taking care of this horse, Johnny," the trainer said in a friendly voice.

"Thank you, Mr. Becker." Johnny stood up straight. He had been working at some dried mud on one of Magic's fetlocks. "I like him a lot," he said, stroking the horse's shining coat. "Almost like he's my own."

"So I guess you wouldn't like it much if you had to stop taking care of him, would you?"

Johnny shook his head. "No, I wouldn't like that at all."

"Good. Because, you see, I like Magic a lot, too. I think he's a great horse—great enough to win the Dogwood Cup next summer." The trainer tugged thoughtfully at his ear. "And I'm going to do whatever I have to do to make sure he gets that chance."

"Yes, sir."

"Red Meyers is a good jockey—one of the best in the business. He's got a damned good reputation with other owners, too. I trust him to give Magic a good ride, and what's more important, Mr. and Mrs. Michaels trust him, also."

"Uh-huh," Johnny mumbled, biting his lip. So that was what the conversation was about, he thought. Red was worried about him. He was probably wondering if he'd really just been walking by the office earlier, or if he had actually been listening in on his phone call. *But what had Red told Mr. Becker?* Johnny wondered.

"It's up to me to make sure Red is happy here," the trainer said, continuing. "And something he told me this afternoon has me concerned."

"Yes, Mr. Becker?"

"He said you'd been sneaking around after him, trying to spy on him. I'd like to hear your side of the story. Care to tell me about it?"

Johnny stared back at the trainer. Red must be really sure of himself, he thought. If he wasn't absolutely sure of where he stood, he never would have taken a chance on talking to Mr. Becker. Johnny knew he had lost—at least for then. The smartest thing would be to keep quiet, in case he got another chance to reveal what he knew about Red.

"Johnny? What's going on?"

"Nothing, sir."

"Nothing?" Johnny shook his head. "Then I have no choice but to believe Red. And if I hear of you bothering him again, I'm going to have to see to it that you're let go. That would mean you'd be banned from the stable. Is that absolutely clear?"

"Yes, sir." Johnny swallowed any further words. He had to stay at Ryan Acres. He couldn't let Mr. Becker fire him. If that happened, he wouldn't be able to protect Magic. "I understand, Mr. Becker."

"Good. But I mean what I said," the trainer said as a warning. "If Red tells me you've been causing him trouble again, out you go."

Johnny nodded. He watched as the trainer walked down the aisle. Taking off his navy knit cap, he ran his hand through his rust-colored

140

hair. "Okay, Red Meyers," he muttered. "If that's how you want to play, that's how we'll play. You think I'm out to prove you're a rat—well, you're right. I am!" He put his hat back on his head. "And I'm not going to let anything keep me from stopping a creep like you!"

11

The two days after Jed's announcement that he wanted to annul their marriage were terrible ones for Caitlin. Most of the time she felt as if she were living a nightmare. If only she could wake up and find Jed lying safely beside her, ready to take her in his arms and kiss her good morning.

Caitlin did her best to appear cheerful, trying hard to be a good hostess for Kathy Michaels. It didn't help, though, that Melanie still refused to speak to her mother. She even walked away whenever she saw her. Frustrated, Caitlin wanted to shake some sense into Melanie. How could she be so stubborn and unyielding? Caitlin wondered. But then her irritation would go away. Even though Melanie was wrong, she understood how she felt.

On the second evening, Dr. Westlake came over to take Mrs. Michaels out to dinner. "I really like her," he told Caitlin when Jed's mother went upstairs to get her coat and purse. "She's a decent, kind woman and I hope that at least one of her children finds a way to forgive her."

"I know, I feel the same way." There was a catch in her voice, and she looked up at him with tears in her eyes. "Oh, Father, I wanted to make everything turn out all right for us. But right now it all seems so hopeless."

"Just remember that old cliché," Dr. Westlake told her, putting an arm around her shoulders. "'It's always darkest before the dawn.' It's true, you know. Don't ever forget it."

"I'll remember," she said and kissed his cheek.

"And that reminds me, I might have some news for you tomorrow afternoon. I've spoken to that doctor from Harvard Medical. He seems quite intelligent."

"And?" Caitlin asked eagerly.

"I have an appointment to see him for an hour tomorrow. I'm going to fly up to Boston for the meeting, and I'll be back late afternoon. I'll come straight here and tell you all about it."

* * *

143

It was nearly five the following afternoon when Dr. Westlake approached the library at Ryan Acres. Caitlin was sitting at her desk, trying to concentrate on some mining business.

"Sorry I'm late," he said, coming into the room. "The planes were backed up and I spent forty-five minutes circling Dulles." He looked over at her and smiled.

"Good news?" Caitlin quickly crossed the room and searched his face with her eyes. "Yes, I can tell it is. Quick, sit down. Tell me everything." She rang for Rollins, who seconds later appeared at the door. "Please bring us some tea, and—" She turned to her father. "Are you hungry? Would you like some cheese and crackers?"

"That would be great, thanks. I missed lunch, and I'm suddenly quite hungry."

Caitlin glanced at Rollins, who nodded and left the room, quietly closing both doors behind him.

"Now, tell me exactly what happened. I can't wait another second. Did you find someone who can help Jed?" she asked as they sat.

"Maybe. Hear me out before you say anything." Caitlin nodded. "I talked to a Dr. Henry Kramer in Boston. Dr. Kramer has developed a new technique that could possibly be used on spine injuries."

"That's wonderful!" Caitlin exclaimed. "When can he see Jed?"

"Now don't get too excited," her father said, putting his hand on her knee. "The method Dr. Kramer has been working on is still very new, and it's extremely risky."

"Risky? How? Do you mean that there's a chance that Jed could die if he has this operation?"

"Well, darling, with any major operation there's always a small possibility that will happen, yes. There's also a chance that something else could go wrong."

"Like what?" she asked.

"Microsurgery is very, very intricate. It's possible that even further damage to the spinal nerves could occur."

"Oh." Caitlin wasn't sure how much worse off Jed could be. Suppose he lost the little bit of feeling he had in his fingers. Wasn't that a risk worth taking?

"The success of the operation depends upon the skill of the surgeon."

"But Dr. Kramer is the best at this microsurgery method, right?"

"Yes, well, he was. But not anymore."

Margaret came into the room carrying a tray, and she set it down on the coffee table in front of them.

"Thank you, Margaret," Caitlin said automatically. Then she turned back to her father. "What do you mean by 'not anymore'?"

"Just that," Dr. Westlake replied. "Dr. Kramer can no longer perform the operation himself. He suffers from Parkinson's disease, and his hands aren't steady enough to do the delicate work the surgery requires."

"Can't someone else do the operation?"

"That's what I was about to tell you. Dr. Kramer has a brilliant assistant whom he feels could perform the operation under his direction. He's a second year resident."

"A resident!" Caitlin said. She shook her head. "No! Absolutely not! There has to be someone else. Someone older, more competent."

"I'm afraid there is no one else. Dr. Kramer said that this young man has been studying with him for six years, since he entered medical school. Dr. Kramer says he not only knows the operation cold, but he has the best hands he's ever seen."

As her father spoke, Caitlin became more and more convinced that she knew of this Dr. Kramer. And she knew his assistant, too. Hoping she was wrong, Caitlin took a deep breath and asked, "Who is this resident? What's his name?"

For a fraction of a second Dr. Westlake hesitated, then answered, "Julian Stokes."

Fifteen minutes later Caitlin was standing by the french doors, looking out. She hadn't said a word. Hearing that Julian was perhaps the only person who could save Jed came as a terrible blow. All she could think was how much Julian hated Jed—and herself.

In her heart, she couldn't help feeling that Julian was evil. Ginny had told her that he had changed, that he was a wonderful doctor now, but Caitlin didn't believe her. And even if he truly cared about the people he treated, would he want to heal Jed? Could she possibly put Jed's life in his hands? Surely the bitterness he must have stored up toward them both over the years would outweigh his desire to heal.

"I don't see how I can let him do it," she said, turning back to face her father, who was still sitting on the sofa.

"I know how you feel about Julian—the hurt he put you through. But that was years ago, Caitlin. People change. The man is a doctor now, a brilliant one according to Dr. Kramer. He's dedicated his life to helping people."

"I understand what you're saying, but I'm just not sure I can bring myself to trust him."

Dr. Westlake rose and went over to his daughter. Putting his hands on her shoulders, he looked directly into her eyes. "Caitlin, I'm afraid you have no other choice. Unless you want Jed to be paralyzed for the rest of his life, you'll have to trust Julian."

"I'm not sure. I need time to think it over."

"Don't take too long. Remember, Jed is in a terrible state of mind. If you wait too long, he may lose his will to live. And no operation will save him then."

Caitlin nodded and looked back out the window.

Caitlin spent a restless night, barely getting an hour's sleep. During the long hours, she thought about the time when she was in love with Julian Stokes—or thought she was, anyway. Julian had been clever and devious, manipulating her into a near disastrous affair. Fortunately, his deception had been discovered before she lost Jed.

Finally the digital clock on the bedside table read 6:00 A.M. She could get up. Rising, she showered, then called the airlines and made a reservation for an early flight to Boston. She decided that she had to see for herself if Julian had really changed. She couldn't accept anyone's word for it. Seeing him herself was the only way.

It was close to eleven o'clock when the taxi dropped her off in front of the hospital where Julian worked. She hadn't told anyone she was coming. She didn't want to give Julian a chance to put on an act for her.

At the hospital's front desk, she was directed to the surgical floor. She stepped off the elevator a few minutes later, and was about to check at the nurses' station when she saw him.

He was talking to a young couple in a waiting room directly in front of her. Even though his back was to her, there was no question in Caitlin's mind that it was Julian. How could she ever forget the way his thick, dark hair curled against the back of his neck? Or the proud way he held his shoulders? In those few seconds it all came back to her—every moment of the months they had been together. Suddenly he was terribly familiar.

Julian appeared to be explaining something to the couple. Gesturing with his hands, he seemed to be outlining some sort of surgical procedure.

Being as unobtrusive as she could, Caitlin quietly stood by the door to the small room. The shock of seeing Julian after so many years began to wear off, and she forced herself to study him objectively. Not wanting to eavesdrop on what

149

was obviously a private talk between the relatives of a patient and their doctor, she listened to the tone of his voice as he spoke with them.

His voice was the same—the quiet, assured, almost mesmerizing voice that had spoken words of love to her. But there was something new, too. There appeared to be genuine concern in his tone. He sounded confident, but not harsh.

"Thank you so very, very much, Dr. Stokes," the man was saying. "You've turned our lives around. We had lost all hope, but now our little girl . . ."

Caitlin had heard enough. Turning, she walked away from the doorway.

She waited near the nurses' station.

Julian saw her the moment he came out of the waiting room. He hesitated slightly as his eyes met hers. Then he stepped toward her.

"Caitlin!" His dark gray eyes were warm and kind. The flinty coldness had disappeared. "Caitlin Ryan. No, excuse me—it's Caitlin Michaels, isn't it." He smiled widely. "It's good to see you."

"Hello, Julian. It's—it's good to see you, too." In her sudden confusion, she was surprised to find herself saying the proper words. "I—I've come to talk to you about Jed."

Julian nodded. "I know. I've been expecting you."

"But I didn't really know until this morning that I was going to come," Caitlin said. But as she looked into his handsome face, she realized that Julian would have heard of her father's visit to Dr. Kramer.

"I have about half an hour before I have to begin afternoon rounds. I, uh, have Jed's X rays in my office, which is just down the hall. Your father brought them. Shall we?" he asked, nodding toward his office. "We can talk there without being interrupted."

Taking her arm, Julian guided her down the corridor and into a neat, sparsely furnished room.

Looking around as she sat down, she realized how well the decor fit Julian. Everything on the desk was neat. A pencil holder, files, a yellow tablet: all were neatly lined up. There were no photographs. There was, however, a painting on the wall opposite the desk. It was a landscape. She looked closer and saw that it was of the hills around Rock Ridge and the road that led down into the town.

"That's to remind me of where I come from," Julian said quietly.

She turned to look at him. Caitlin was sure

151

that her surprise showed on her face. Julian had always hidden from everyone the fact that he was a miner's son. But now he had this painting hanging on the wall.

"I've changed, Caitlin," he admitted, smiling with deep sincerity. "And"—he hesitated, took a breath, then went on—"you started that change. When I lost you, I realized that I'd done a lot of terrible things. Lying to you was wrong, but lying to myself was even worse. Now I've accepted who I am, and I'm proud of that. I'm never again going to pretend I'm someone I'm not."

"Julian—" Caitlin said, unable to continue because she was overwhelmed with emotion.

"But all those terrible things I did to you, all of the lies I told you, the way I hated you ever while I was falling in love with you—"

"Julian, don't. It was a long time ago."

"No, Caitlin, I have to say this." He reached out to touch her, but stopped and put his hand on the edge of the desk instead. "What I'm trying to say is that I would do anything in the world to make up for the way I hurt you. Maybe by operating on Jed I'd have that chance."

"Yes, that's why I came here." She had decided. She did want Julian to operate.

"I have to be honest with you," he said. "The operation is still considered experimental."

"My father explained that to me."

"Did he explain how serious the operation is, and the possible consequences if something should go wrong?" He hesitated, then put his hand on hers. "Jed—"

"Could die? I know."

"Actually, I was thinking of further paralysis. But, yes, there is always the possibility that a patient could die during an operation of this magnitude."

"I understand." Closing her eyes, Caitlin nodded. She opened her eyes again. "Thank you for being honest with me. Will you do the operation?"

"I'll need Jed's permission."

Yes, that was something she had to deal with—getting Jed to put his life in the hands of his worst enemy.

12

Feeling the need for some private time to prepare herself to face Jed, Caitlin had breakfast
alone in her room.

Later, dressed in dark green wool slacks and a
matching cashmere sweater, she looked at herself in the mirror. The outfit needed a bit more
color, she decided. Going over to her dresser,
she opened her scarf drawer and was about to
take out her favorite—a red scarf with a green
print—when she noticed a yellow one. Jed had
bought the scarf for her in Hawaii.

Her throat tightened and she felt tears sting
the back of her eyes when she thought of that
happy day.

"Stop it!" Caitlin told herself firmly. Just stop
feeling sorry for yourself—and for Jed. There are
a lot of happy days ahead. For both of you.

Determined, she picked up the yellow scarf and walked back to the mirror. After knotting the large square of bright silk casually around her shoulders, she stepped back to see how it looked.

"There," she said. "That's much better." Picking up her tan bag, she went downstairs.

Melanie was waiting for her in the hall. When Caitlin had returned from Boston the day before, she told both Melanie and Mrs. Michaels about Julian.

"I just wanted to wish you luck," Melanie told her. Her voice was filled with emotion. "Oh, Caitlin, I do hope that you can convince him to give his permission—"

She was interrupted by the sound of the door chimes.

"I wonder who that can be," Caitlin said. She turned to Melanie. "Were you expecting anyone this early?"

"No." Melanie shook her head.

Caitlin shrugged. "I'll get it. Maybe it's a delivery person," she said on her way to the door.

A man in a suit said, "Mrs. Michaels? Mrs. Jed Michaels?"

"Yes?" Suddenly she felt frightened. The man looked so serious. Something had happened to

Jed, she thought wildly. They didn't want to tell her over the phone, so they sent someone to tell her in person. *But, no—that would be silly,* she thought. Finally Caitlin said, "Yes, I'm Mrs. Michaels."

"This is for you." Reaching into his inside coat pocket, the man took out a business-sized envelope and handed it to her.

"But—" Caitlin looked down at the envelope, then back up at the man to ask what it was. But he was already hurrying down the steps. Mystified, she watched him get into his car and drive away.

"Who was that?" Melanie asked, standing beside Caitlin as she closed the door.

"I haven't the slightest idea." Caitlin held out the envelope. "He gave me this."

"Who's it from? What is it?

"Let's see." Caitlin turned the envelope over so she could see the address in the upper left-hand corner. "'Wood and Wood, Attorneys-at-Law.'"

"Oh, lawyers," Melanie said with a shrug. "Probably Ryan Mining business."

"Not hand delivered," Caitlin replied. Turning the envelope over again, she opened it and pulled out the pages inside. She unfolded the sheets of paper, and after a long moment she looked up at Melanie. "I guess I should have expected this." She handed Melanie the papers with a shaking hand. "Jed told me he was going to do it."

"Do what?" Melanie took the papers, but didn't look at them. "What did Jed say he was going to do?"

"He said he was going to file for an annulment," Caitlin said, her voice flat and dull.

"An annulment?" Melanie gasped. "You mean that Jed wants to dissolve your marriage? Just end it?"

Caitlin nodded. "As if it never happened."

"But that's awful!" Melanie exclaimed. "How could he do such a thing?" She glanced down at the papers in her hand, then up at Caitlin. "What are you going to do?" she asked.

"I'm going to put a stop to this, that's what." Taking back the papers, she stuffed them into her purse. "Right now!"

Caitlin did not enter Jed's room quietly that time. Yanking the door open, she marched over to his bed and dropped the papers on it.

"Just what are you trying to prove, Jed?" she demanded, her voice filled with fury.

"We've been through this," Jed said, jerking his head around to look at her. "And you don't have a choice now. When those papers were delivered and you accepted them, that was it. See you in court."

"Oh, no, you don't!" Her eyes narrowed. "You think you've got everything all figured out, but you're wrong. You're forgetting that I've got two lawyers working for me. Did you think I couldn't call them?"

"Corporate lawyers," Jed said. "What do they know?"

"How much law do you have to know to understand an annulment?"

"Okay, so you have lawyers," Jed replied. "They must have told you that this is the best way. By dissolving our marriage, there won't be any legal problems dividing our money, property, Ryan Mining, your other holdings. But if you want a divorce instead . . ." He let his words trail off.

"I don't want either," Caitlin said firmly. "I love you, Jed. I'm your wife, and I intend to stay your wife. *'Until death do us part.'* Isn't that what we promised each other?"

Jed's eyes filled with tears, and he turned away. Oh, God, how he loved her. And, yes, he had meant those words. He would still mean them if it weren't for his injury.

"Everything is different now, Caitlin. I'm not

the man you married. I'm a cripple, and I'll be that way for the rest of my life. And not even in a wheelchair, but flat on my back like this." His voice was heavy with anguish. "Don't you understand, nothing works. My body is dead."

"Listen to me, Jed, there may be some hope," Caitlin said softly. "That's what I've come to tell you." She picked up the annulment papers and put them aside on the bed table, away from her sight. Pulling her chair closer to Jed, she took his hand. "They've developed a new operation that might be able to help you."

Jed stared at her in disbelief, a momentary flash of hope came into his eyes. "It can't be," he said. "The doctors have told me there's no chance for recovery. The best they say I could hope for would be some minimal movement of my hands, and that's only a long shot. No one has ever mentioned an operation."

"There is one, but it's new and very risky. A doctor in Boston has been working to perfect it."

"Does he know about my case?" Jed could hardly allow himself to believe this glimmer of hope.

"Yes, he knows all about you."

"And he'll operate on me?"

"He said he would take you on, but there are tremendous risks you have to know about. It's a very dangerous operation."

159

"I'm not afraid of death, Caitlin. Living like this is worse than anything for me, I don't care what the risks are. I want that operation. When can he do it?"

"We can arrange to fly you to Boston in an air ambulance tomorrow. The operation can be performed by the end of the week."

"Tell him I'm ready to go now, Caitlin." Jed's dejection turned to grim determination.

"There's something else, Jed, something important."

"What is it?"

Caitlin took a deep breath, and, summoning all her courage, told him the name of the doctor.

"Julian Stokes!" Jed exploded. "Never! How could you expect me to allow him of all people, to operate on me. He's my enemy. He hates me!"

"But Jed, he's the only one who can do this procedure. There is no one else."

"There must be."

"There isn't, Jed. Please trust me. My father has searched all over."

"It isn't you I don't trust, Caitlin," Jed said with a heavy sigh of sadness. His one chance at life was being stolen from him. How could she ask him to trust Julian Stokes?

Jed looked at the beautiful face of the woman he loved, and remembered how obsessed Julian had been with her. Could he possibly put his life in the hands of a man who hated him so for loving Caitlin? It wasn't possible. At best, the operation was dangerous and uncertain. If Jed didn't survive, Julian would have Caitlin all to himself. He cringed at the thought, his old jealousy beginning to boil to the surface. Even now, when his very life depended on this operation, he found himself overwhelmed by the idea of Caitlin and Julian together.

"There has to be someone else," he said in desperation.

"There isn't, Jed. Listen to me, please. Julian's changed. He's not the same person we used to know."

"People don't really change, not that much," Jed answered, sinking back hopelessly against the pillow. "Not someone like Julian Stokes, anyway.

"All he ever wanted was revenge, and now he's found a way. Well, he's wrong. His plan isn't going to work."

"That's not true, Jed," Caitlin pleaded. "Please, you must let him operate."

"Never!"

"He's the only one who can do it. He's your only chance. Our only chance."

Jed was adamant. There was no way he was going to let Julian Stokes touch him.

Frantic, desperate to find a way to get through Jed's stubborn fury, Caitlin used the last possible argument she had to convince him.

"You must have the operation," she said, "not just for yourself, but for us, Jed, for me and for our baby."

"Our baby?"

"Yes," she said firmly. "I'm pregnant, Jed."

Jed was stunned. "Why didn't you tell me?"

"I was going to tell you last week, but," she broke off. If only she had told him then, there probably wouldn't be any need for an operation. Jed wouldn't be in the hospital, because he certainly wouldn't have gone surfing if he knew he was going to be a father. "Jed, please," she pleaded, "the baby and I need you."

Turning his head towards the window, Jed stared out in silence. Long moments passed before he turned back to face her. "All right," he said, "I'll have the operation, but only on one condition."

"Anything you want Jed, just say yes."

"I'll have the operation, but if it isn't a success, you'll agree to the annulment."

"No, Jed."

"And there'll be no baby either."

"I can't . . ."

"You must, Caitlin, because I swear to you I

will never be your crippled husband. Never! Nor will I be a father who can't even hold his own child. Absolutely not. I promise you I will not have that operation unless you agree to my conditions. And, if you love me as you say you do, you'll do it my way."

Caitlin stared at him in horror. She did love him with all her heart, but he was asking the impossible. He was asking her to choose between him and their unborn child.

Caitlin looked at Jed, at this man who meant everything in her life, and who, without this operation, would spend the rest of his life in misery, physically and emotionally destroyed— barely alive. If only she had spoken sooner about the baby, she might have saved him. It was a secret she had no right to have kept, even for a day. And she alone had to answer for that mistake, for she alone held his chance at life. In agony, she wrestled with the dilemma.

Then she knew what she had to do. For now, she would say the words he wanted to hear. "Yes," she whispered. "I promise."

13

With Dr. Westlake's help, Caitlin quickly made the arrangements to have Jed moved to Boston and admitted to the hospital the following day.

Though the flight was difficult and uncomfortable, Caitlin comforted Jed and sat with him, holding his hand all the way. When the small jet landed, they were met by an ambulance, and taken directly to a private suite at the hospital.

A series of tests were given the next day, and the operation scheduled for the following morning.

Never once, during those painful days, was the terrible promise mentioned, though the weight of it was nearly crushing Caitlin. Alone in her hotel room the night before the operation, she could think of little else. Finally, her thoughts became so oppressive that she jumped up from her bed, threw on her clothes and fled the room.

Walking aimlessly through downtown Boston, she saw little of the city, her mind was spinning too wildly. First the baby, then Jed, and finally Julian.

Could she really trust Julian with Jed's life? What if she was wrong about him? What if he had lied to her about being different now, about wanting to have that painting in his office so he would be reminded that he couldn't run away from who he was? What if all of that was nothing but a gigantic lie? He had deceived her before—could this be just another of his tricks?

Hatred's power consumes people, destroying them over time. Julian had hated her and Jed for so many years. Was he still obsessed with hurting her? She didn't think so, but how could she know for certain?

She had observed him carefully since their arrival, looking for signs of the old Julian. Of course, he knew she would be watching him, and he was so clever.

No more, she told herself, she mustn't let her mind run away with these tortured thoughts. Her other preoccupation was equally tormenting. She dared not consider the child within her and the dreadful promise she had made.

Finally, exhausted from her agonizing deliberations, she turned back towards the hotel. Once in her room, she undressed listlessly, and got into to bed to wait for the relief of sleep. Still, the respite she so deeply desired wouldn't come.

Hours passed with no abatement from the thoughts spinning in her mind. At last, somewhere in the early pre-dawn hours, she drifted off, only to be awakened by the most terrifying nightmares. Frightening dreams of monsters tearing at her very insides, hideous pictures of death and destruction.

At six o'clock, a very weary Caitlin dragged herself from her bed. She showered and dressed and sat down to wait for the full morning to come. This day would tell her what would happen to the rest of her life.

By seven o'clock Caitlin Ryan Michaels knew what she had to do. She'd made her decision, one that was final and irreversible.

She would have to tell Jed right now, before his operation. She would go to him and tell him that she couldn't fulfill her promise. She wouldn't. No matter what the consequences, she was going to have their child. She had to get to the hospital quickly, before they took him down for the surgery.

The operation was scheduled for seven thirty. If she hurried, she could make it to the hospital in time.

In the lobby of the hotel, she waved off the doorman's offer to hail her a cab. It was only a few blocks. She would get there faster on foot.

A few minutes later, frantic and breathless, she got off the elevator on Jed's floor. The first person she saw was Dr. Westlake.

"Whoa, honey. Calm down," he said, putting his hands on her shoulders. "Jed's already in the operating room and everything's going well."

"But—but I didn't get to talk to him," she moaned.

"Please don't worry. Jed was sedated early this morning. Even if you'd gotten here an hour ago, he probably wouldn't have known who you were." He patted her shoulder, trying to comfort her.

"You don't understand. I needed to talk to him," she said, tears welling up in her eyes.

"Look, Jed is going to come through this operation with flying colors. You'll probably even be able to talk to him this afternoon."

She nodded numbly.

"Now," he said, leading her to a couch in the

small waiting area, "why don't you sit here and I'll go get you a cup of coffee. Or would you like tea instead?"

"Herbal tea," she told him, thinking about the baby.

When he had brought it, Caitlin held the hot tea cupped in her hands until it cooled. Taking a sip, she glanced up at the clock on the wall. She looked back down at the tea for a moment, then back at the clock. Never before had time dragged by so slowly. Sometime later, Dr. Westlake excused himself to make a call to check on one of his own patients. When he returned, Caitlin got up and walked the length of the corridor. Stopping, she looked out a window for several minutes, staring out at the city below. Then she turned and walked back to the couch.

"I don't think I can stand one more minute of this waiting. It's been so long. Is there any way you can check to see what's happening? Please?"

"I know it seems like a long time, Caitlin," he said gently. "But it really hasn't been." Suddenly he looked up as a person in hospital greens stopped in front of them. It was Julian.

Caitlin looked up at the same time, her eyes searching the surgeon's face. "Is Jed . . . ?" She couldn't finish the sentence.

"He's doing fine," Julian said. She looked up

into his eyes and saw nothing but kindness there. "As far as we're concerned, the operation was a success."

"Oh, thank God," Caitlin whispered, sighing with relief. "When can I see him?"

"He's in recovery now, but he's still out," Julian said. He took her hand and gave it a gentle squeeze. "I'd rather you wait until he returns to his room to see him. It'll be in about three hours."

"You said the operation was a success," Dr. Westlake said. "Do you really think that Jed will regain the full use of his legs?"

"We won't really know the extent of Jed's recovery for some time. There's some healing that must occur, and the swelling must go down. Then there will be the physical therapy, of course."

"What are you saying?" Caitlin asked. "Is Jed going to be all right or not?"

"Honestly, we just don't know. We won't know for some time. But don't worry, Caitlin." Julian's expression relaxed. "I'm a good surgeon, and everything went extremely well. I have every reason to believe it won't be long before Jed is walking again."

"Thank you, Julian—for everything."

"You're welcome." Julian reached out and

took her hand, then held it long enough to tell her in a low, sincere voice, "And thank you, Caitlin, for giving me a second chance." He kissed her cheek, turned and walked away.

After he left, Dr. Westlake looked at Caitlin curiously. "I guess I won't ask what that was about," he said after a moment. "You look happy, and that's all that matters to me."

"Thank you for not asking," she said. "Someday, I promise, I'll tell you the whole story."

"Okay," he said, nodding. "And now that things are going so well, I really must catch the next plane home."

"Bye." She hugged him. "And remember, I love you."

"I can feel my toes!" Jed announced in an amazed tone four days later as Caitlin entered his room.

"Really?" She was just as excited. "You can honestly feel them?"

"You bet I can!" he assured her happily. "Dr. Kramer was in earlier and he tested me. He said it definitely isn't my imagination."

"That's terrific," Caitlin said with a distracted nod. She remembered how Julian had told her it would be better if Jed didn't see him. It might upset him. So Dr. Kramer was doing the follow-up exams.

Jed didn't notice her pause, going on delightedly, "Dr. Kramer also said that if I keep on doing this well, I should be out of here in another week. He's arranging for a therapist to come back to Ryan Acres and work with me there. That means I can get back to managing the horses—especially Magic—sooner than I'd hoped."

"That's wonderful, Jed."

"And, Caitlin—" His expression sobered. I've been doing a lot of thinking lately, and—"

"And?" she asked, instantly fearful.

He smiled. "Don't look at me that way. I want to apologize to you about what I made you promise about the baby. I didn't mean it—not really." Caitlin nodded, her eyes filling with tears. "And, if it's not too late, I've realized that you were right about my mother. I didn't think people could change, but I should have known better. You've changed from the way you were years ago at Highgate. When I met you, you were a selfish flirt. And now . . ." Jed's eyes were shining with love. "And Julian changed, too. I have to give my mother a chance to show that she has, too."

"Jed, you mean it?"

"Yes, I do," he said sincerely. "If she'll forgive me, that is."

"Oh, Jed, I'm so happy you feel that way. Melanie's beginning to come around, too. And your mother really does care about you. Very much." She glanced down for a second, then back up. "I have a confession to make. Remember that day in the hospital, when your mother flew in from California and you refused to see her?" He nodded.

"Well, I asked her to stay at Ryan Acres for a while. At least until after your operation. I like her, Jed. She's been a big comfort to me during these past few days."

"You said she was only going to stay until after the operation," Jed said, suddenly distressed. "Has she left already? Is she back in California?"

"No," Caitlin said. "She's still here. She's planning to leave from Logan Airport at four."

"You mean she's here—in Boston?"

"Actually, she's right down the hall. She wanted a chance to see you one more time—to say goodbye."

"Oh, how stupid I've been. Ever since the accident, all I've done is hurt the people who love me: you, Melanie, and my mother, too."

"Why don't I go get her?" Caitlin said.

172

"Yes, please." Jed took a deep, steadying breath. "Please tell her I want to see her."

Caitlin went to the door. Opening it, she beckoned to her mother-in-law. As Mrs. Michaels came in, Caitlin backed out.

"Jed?" the older woman whispered, not knowing what to expect.

"Mom?"

Caitlin saw the look of joy in Jed's mother's eyes as he spoke. "Hello, Jed—oh, my baby!"

Quietly, Caitlin slipped from the room and closed the door behind her.

14

Jed was home in time for Thanksgiving. At Caitlin's request, Mrs. Michaels had agreed to stay on at Ryan Acres through the holidays so that she might have a chance to get reacquainted with her children.

Dr. Westlake was there as well. And so was Howard Josso. "It looks as though he's going to be an official member of the family before long, anyway," Caitlin told Melanie when she asked if he could come to Thanksgiving dinner. "So by all means ask him to join us."

Caitlin had been absolutely right. A week before Christmas, Howard presented Melanie with an exquisite diamond and emerald engagement ring. When they told Caitlin, she insisted that the traditional Christmas Eve celebration be turned into an engagement party. During a quiet moment just after the party, Caitlin said to Howard, "I'm so very happy for you both. I couldn't ask for a better brother-in-law. You know I love her very much; almost as though she were my real sister."

"And I love her, too," Howard replied, smiling widely. "I just hope we'll be as happy as you and Jed are."

"I hope so, too," she answered, meaning it. "We're all so very lucky."

Jed's Christmas present to Caitlin was a chestnut filly. "She'll be a yearling next week, on January first," he said as Caitlin unwrapped a silver-framed photograph of the lovely young Thoroughbred. "I kind of thought Magic might need a stablemate—a racing stablemate." He grinned. "You know, to keep him on his toes."

"You mean the way I keep you on your toes?" she asked, teasing him. Jed's second present to her was throwing away the two canes he had been using to help him walk.

"I want to take you dancing on New Year's Eve," he said, beaming proudly as he walked unaided across the floor.

"And I'm going to hold you to it," Caitlin told

him, slipping her arms around him and kissing him.

It was snowing when they drove Mrs. Michaels to Washington to catch her plane back to California. Since Jed wasn't allowed to drive yet and Caitlin had promised not to drive during bad weather until after the baby was born, the three of them rode to Dulles in the back of the Bentley. Jed's mother sat between Jed and Caitlin, talking the whole way.

"Just think, Mom," Jed commented, "in another few hours you'll be basking in southern California sunshine."

"Thank goodness. But," she added, "I wouldn't trade all the sunshine in the world for the last couple of months." She covered his hand with her own. "Your accident was a terrible, terrible tragedy, and I would give anything for it not to have happened. But at the same time, it did bring us back together. I'm grateful for that."

At the airport, just before she boarded the plane, Mrs. Michaels turned to Caitlin and hugged her. "Thank you for everything, dear. If it hadn't been for you, I wouldn't have Jed and Melanie back." She kissed Caitlin's cheek warmly. "And you have Jed call me just the moment that my grandchild decides to make his—or her—entrance. Promise?"

"I will," Caitlin said. "I promise."

Caitlin and Jed waited until the plane had cleared the landing strip before they headed back to the car.

"I hope your mother can come back sometime next summer," Caitlin said. "I think she'd really like spending time with the baby."

"I'd like to spend more time with her, too," Jed said. "We have so much lost time to make up for."

"Let's try always to remember that, Jed." Caitlin slipped an arm around his waist as they walked. "Time really is precious, and you can never, ever get it back once it's gone."

Jed nodded solemnly. "I'll remember."

Most of Magic's training was completed by the end of January, and Lou Becker arranged to have him enter his first race.

"The purse is a small one," he told Jed and Caitlin. "But it doesn't really matter. Actually this will be more like a dress rehearsal than a real race. It'll give us the opportunity to see how he handles himself on a track with other horses. We also need to find out how he's going to handle the noise and excitement of the crowd. Some very gifted horses never learn to deal with it." He shook his head. "Anyway, don't expect a lot this first time. Just be happy if he gets in there and finishes the race with a reasonably good time."

Magic surprised them all, however, by coming in first. He was a good two lengths ahead of the second place horse.

Jed and Caitlin celebrated by going out to dinner with Caitlin's father. "Lou couldn't believe it when Magic crossed the finish line first," Jed told Dr. Westlake, a wide grin splitting his face. "I was pretty excited myself. I know I was jumping up and down as he came down the stretch. Just ask Caitlin."

"Well, I would have been jumping myself," Caitlin said. "But I'm not doing a lot of that these days." She patted her huge stomach fondly. "But I'm really glad now that we entered him in the Dogwood Cup in July."

"Then it's on to the Derby next year," Jed announced.

"The Derby?" Dr. Westlake repeated as he glanced from Jed to Caitlin, then back to Jed. "Are you talking about the *Kentucky* Derby?"

"The very one!" Jed said, laughing delighted-ly. "Ryan Acres Stables is going to be one very successful stable after Magic wins it next year."

"Let's just get him through the Dogwood first," Caitlin said cautiously.

"Don't worry, darling," Jed replied as he picked up his wineglass and took a sip. "With Lou training him, and Red riding him, how can Magic do anything but win?"

Johnny was proud of Magic, too, and he bragged to all his friends about the horse. "You just wait," he told them. "He'll be better than all those other famous racehorses like Man O'War and Citation and Seattle Slew. Magic isn't just fast, he's got what really counts—he's got heart."

But while Johnny was happy that Magic had won, and he knew that the ride Red Meyers had given the horse had a lot to do with Magic's win, he still didn't trust the jockey. He had no real proof, though. There was just that one phone call he couldn't forget.

He knew he'd have to continue watching Red, waiting for him to make a real slip. Then Johnny could do something. He wasn't sure what, but when it was time Johnny was sure he'd know what to do.

Lou continued to enter Magic in smaller races throughout the spring. The colt won all but two. Neither loss, Johnny hated to admit, appeared to be Red's fault. In one race, Magic had been boxed in by other horses at the very beginning, and had never been able to get completely free. The other time he had had a slight bruise on the bottom of one foot which wasn't discovered until after the race. Still, in spite of his injury, Magic had come in third.

At the end of May, Lou and Jed decided to give the horse a much-needed rest in order to prepare him for the Dogwood Cup in mid-July.

Jed and Caitlin were sitting by the pool one morning in early June. They could see the pasture from where their chaise longues were situated. Caitlin sat up to put more oil on her legs.

Recapping the bottle, she put it on the table beside her, then leaned back and shielded her eyes from the sun. She smiled as she watched Magic and the chestnut filly Jed had given her for Christmas race across the lush green grass.

"Umm." She let out a long happy sigh and dropped her hand away to turn and look at Jed. "I never thought my life would be this wonderful." She reached out and trailed her finger along his tanned arm. "I can't imagine being happier than I am at this moment."

"What about when the baby's born?" Jed put his hand gently on her stomach. Suddenly he grinned. "He just kicked me."

"Um-hmm," she said with a laugh. "I felt *her*, too."

"You know I really think it's about time we decided on names for *him*—or her." He leaned over and kissed Caitlin, then settled on his elbow, facing her. "What do you think?"

"Well, if it's a boy, he'll be Jed, of course."

"But we won't call him Junior, will we? I've always thought that sounded kind of dumb."

"No. We'll think of something else. But I do want to name our first boy after you."

"Our *first* boy?" Jed asked, sounding surprised. "Are you planning another one already?"

"Sort of," she replied. "I hated being an only child. I was hoping we could have two boys and a girl. How does that sound?"

"Sounds fine, but it's not like you can just plan it that way." Caitlin scowled. "Okay, have it your way. What do you want to name the girl?"

"Well, I have been doing a bit of thinking about that," she admitted. "There are so many names to choose from, but there's one name that's most special to me."

"And what's that?"

"Laura," Caitlin said quietly. "My mother's name. If you wouldn't really mind, I'd like to name a daughter after her."

"I think that would be wonderful," Jed answered. "And I know your father would love it, too."

Caitlin was lying propped up in bed in her private room on the maternity floor. Her baby had been born early that morning, June twenty-eighth, at 7:10 A.M.

She held the baby cradled in her arms. Entering the room with a shy smile, Jed walked toward them. He was holding out a huge pink teddy bear. *As if we don't have enough pink around here*, Caitlin thought. Though it had only been a couple of hours since the baby was born, the room was already filled with flowers—all pink.

"I think that's a little too big for her," Caitlin said with a happy laugh as Jed put the bear down on a nearby chair. "It must be at least nine times as large as she is."

"Then I'll get her nine small ones," Jed said. "Whatever she wants."

"Well, I think what she would like right now is

182

to get acquainted with her father." As she spoke, Caitlin gently pulled the edge of the pink blanket away from the tiny perfect face.

"Hello there, Laura," Jed said in an awed whisper.

She seemed to look up at Jed, then yawned and closed her eyes.

"I really bowled her over, huh?"

"No, it's just that she feels comfortable with you," Caitlin answered with a smile.

"She's so beautiful," Jed said as he tentatively reached out and ever so carefully touched the dark silky hair that covered the baby's head. "She looks like you."

"I think she looks like you," Caitlin replied. "She has your strong chin. I can tell already that she's going to be a very determined young lady."

"And with those looks, maybe we should start worrying about all those broken hearts she'll leave behind."

"Umm, maybe." Caitlin grinned. "Maybe what she's going to need are a couple of brothers to keep her in line."

"Still want to have those two boys you mentioned?"

"Absolutely."

"We'll have to have a serious talk about that when Laura is a bit older."

"Right." Caitlin looked up at him, her eyes dancing. "I was thinking that a second honeymoon might be a good idea—in October. Maybe Hawaii again?"

"Terrific!" Jed leaned over and very quietly, so as not to disturb the baby, kissed Caitlin. "I can hardly wait."

15

The day of the Dogwood Cup finally arrived. Magic had been brought to the track the night before, and Johnny stayed near his stall all night.

Throughout the week before the race, Johnny had watched Red carefully, ready to turn him in if he did anything even vaguely suspicious. But Red had done nothing, and Johnny was beginning to wonder if he had been wrong about the jockey all along. Still, he told himself, he would have to stay alert.

Leaving Magic only long enough to go to the catering truck for breakfast, Johnny was returning now to the stall. He stopped walking when he heard Red speaking to a man in the tack room next to Magic's stall. What attracted Johnny was that the two men were speaking in low tones, as if they didn't want to be overheard.

Tossing the rest of his sweet roll into a trash barrel, Johnny silently crept up to the door and listened. He could barely make out the words, but when he pressed his face against the wooden wall and peered through a crack, he could see the face of the man to whom Red was talking.

Johnny scowled when he recognized Avil Horton. Mr. Horton was a big man in the racing world. In fact, he even had a horse of his own entered in the race that day. What was he doing talking to Red? Johnny wondered.

There was only one answer that Johnny could think of—that Avil Horton was asking Red to throw the race so his own horse could win. Desperately, he tried to hear what they were saying. He had to be certain.

"Okay, Mr. Horton," Red said as he shoved some money into his pocket. "That's five thousand dollars now, and another five after the race."

"You got it!" Horton said. "And I don't want any slip-ups. I just want your horse to lose. Understand?"

"Look, I know what I'm doing, okay? I've ridden that horse in six races now, so I know how to handle him. I know just where to slow him down so it looks like he's tiring naturally. He'll lose, all right. Oh, he won't lose big. After all, I've got my reputation to consider, too. But he'll definitely be out of the money."

"That's all I care about," Horton said.

"One more thing—how do I know you're going to come through with the rest of the money?"

"And how do I know you won't take the five I gave you just now and go ahead and win the race? As you just pointed out, your reputation is at stake. How can I be sure you'll lose for me?"

"Because I need that other five, and I need it bad. I've got—well, let's just say, obligations."

"Then I guess we'll just have to trust each other, won't we?" Horton said smoothly.

"Yeah, right."

Johnny had heard enough, and he didn't want to be caught listening when the two of them left the room. He quickly moved away.

What was he going to do? he wondered. Leaning against a paddock railing trying to appear casual, he watched as Red and Avil Horton left the building, each going his own way.

If he went to Lou with the story, the trainer would probably say he was trying to make trouble for Red again. He'd probably be fired right on the spot. As Red had told Horton, he had a reputation for winning. He was riding a top horse. Anyone in that position would be foolish to throw a race. No, Lou wouldn't believe him.

What if he approached Mr. and Mrs. Michaels? No, not Mrs. Michaels—she was kind of like a queen, or something. He wouldn't even know how to begin to talk to her. Every time she so much as said "good morning" or "good afternoon," he became tongue-tied. But Mr. Michaels was a regular guy. He'd even grown up on a ranch out west. But would he believe his story any more than Lou would? Red had been doing a good job for them so far, so why would he stop now? No, Johnny knew he couldn't go to Mr. Michaels, either.

Okay, then, what about the racing officials? Johnny thought about it for a few minutes, then came to the conclusion that that, too, was out. Red had probably already stashed the money in some hiding place. What kind of proof would he have against the jockey except his word? As for Horton? Oh, sure he could just imagine the disbelief on the faces of the officials if he tried to say something about one of the most influential racehorse owners in Virginia. On the East Coast, for that matter.

But he had to do something. He couldn't let Magic down.

But what?

All at once Johnny knew—he knew exactly what he had to do.

The race was just about to begin. The horses were being brought into the paddock, where they would be saddled by the trainers themselves, in front of a crowd of spectators.

From a hiding place near the entrance to the jockeys' dressing room, Johnny watched as Magic was led in by another groom. In order to put his plan into action, he had told Lou Becker he was sick so the trainer had assigned another groom to Magic.

Now Johnny slipped into the dressing room. It was crowded with jockeys changing into their silks for the next race. Spotting Red, Johnny took a deep breath and forced himself to walk up to Red.

"I've got a message for you, Red," he said.

"Huh!" Red stared at him. "What are you talking about, kid? And what are you doing here? You ought to know no one's allowed in here except jockeys and race officials. You're not either of those, so scram."

"The message is from Avil Horton," Johnny said nervously.

"What?" Red's eyes narrowed to slits. "How do you know about Horton?"

"Does it matter?" Johnny looked back, unblinking. "Do you want to hear the message, or not?"

"Yeah, okay," Red hissed. "And for God's sake lower your voice." He motioned to some of the jockeys who were now starting to file out of the room. "But hurry."

"I don't think we should talk here. Someone might hear. Come into the bathroom." He turned and walked toward the adjoining empty room, hoping that Red would automatically follow, too.

"Oh, okay," Red grumbled and followed Johnny. "But make it snappy, I've got to get go—"

He never got the rest of the words out. As soon as he was inside the room, Johnny swiveled around and swung at Red. His fist connected with Red's jaw, and the jockey went down in a heap on the floor.

In minutes Johnny had changed into Red's clothes—the breeches, boots, and Ryan Acres silks.

Leaving Red lying on the floor, Johnny pulled the racing cap down firmly over his forehead so that the brim shadowed his eyes and much of his face. Then he hurried from the room.

He was going to ride Magic, Johnny thought, filled with awe. He could do it. He knew he could. He had ridden Magic dozens of times when the colt was being breezed. He knew how to handle him. He could ride him in his sleep. Hadn't he done so often, at least in his dreams?

But first Johnny had to get through the official preliminaries. That would be tough. But if he kept his head down, he just might get away with it. If no one looked directly into his face, he did look enough like Red to be mistaken for him. That fact was what had given him the idea.

He weighed in and had weights added to Magic's saddle pad without a hitch. He'd hesitated only once, but then one of the jockeys behind him had given him a friendly shove and said, "Get with it, Red." And Johnny knew he had succeeded in fooling at least one person.

It gave him the needed confidence to walk over to where Magic and Lou were waiting, hand the saddle to Becker, and wait while the man fastened the girth. Then Becker turned to Johnny and gave him a lift into the saddle.

When the trainer looked up to give him last-minute instructions, Johnny kept his face covered by adjusting his goggles. Becker didn't seem to notice anything unusual and Johnny let out a sigh of relief as the trainer put an easy hand on Johnny's leg. "Okay, Red, just ride him the way you did during the last race. Keep him steady until you get to that far post. Then, as soon as you've got a clear space, give him his head. He'll do the rest. And remember, don't use the whip. He doesn't like the whip."

Johnny nodded his understanding while keeping his head averted. The trainer gave Magic a friendly slap on the rump and stepped back.

He had done it, Johnny told himself as he and Magic were led out of the paddock toward the track. He had done it! Now all that was left was to give Magic the best ride he could. Hopefully they would win. But even if they didn't, at least Magic would have a fair chance to win.

As soon as they entered the starting gate and were shut in, Johnny leaned forward and gave Magic an encouraging pat on the neck. "It's okay, boy. We're going to show everyone that you can win and I can ride."

The bell rang, the electronic gates snapped open with a clang, and they were off. Magic leapt forward, sending them well in front of the pack. Johnny hadn't been quite ready, and he was a bit off balance. One foot had slipped partially out of the stirrup.

But as the colt settled down into his powerful stride, Johnny righted himself and leaned out well over Magic's neck. Winding his hands tighter through the reins, he got the feel of Magic's mouth and let his hands move with the horse. They were working in perfect harmony. *We'll do it together—together.* . . . The thought pounded through Johnny's mind with each thud of Magic's hooves.

From the corner of his eye, he saw another horse moving up beside them. That was all right. Just as long as they didn't pass and then box Magic in. *Steady.* Johnny remembered that Lou had said to keep Magic steady. Johnny did his best, and he could feel the colt responding, the muscles in his shoulders checking slightly.

That's right, Johnny mentally told Magic. *We've got a way to go. Let that horse set the pace for us.*

They rounded the first turn. Johnny chanced it and took a quick look behind him. Except for the other horse beside them, all the others were at least a length behind.

They rounded the next turn. There was the long straightaway in front of them now. The other horse was moving slightly ahead. Johnny saw the jockey going for the whip, striking the horse—one, two, three.

The horse responded, leaping ahead. First by only half a length, then a whole length in front.

But soon he felt Magic respond to being left behind. He saw and felt Magic's muscles answer as he stretched out his stride. They caught up, galloping neck and neck.

They were nearing the far pole. There was only the final bend, then it was a short distance to the finish line.

The other horse's jockey raised his whip again, and down it came, again and again. The horse tried, but he was tiring. Johnny could see the flecks of foam flying from his nostrils, the lather building on his neck.

They rounded the bend. The rest of the pack was almost two lengths behind. The other horse began slipping back. Yet, amazingly, Magic still was fresh. It was as if he were out in the pastures back at Ryan Acres and was running just for fun.

They had reached the final pole. The finish line was ahead. "Now," Johnny called to Magic. He gave the colt his head, leaning far forward and loosening the reins enough so that Magic wasn't hampered by any pressure from his hands.

It was as if Magic were flying. Johnny barely stayed on top as Magic tore down the track alone. When he crossed the finish line, he was nearly four lengths ahead of the rest.

The crowd was still cheering wildly as Johnny stood up in the stirrups and gradually brought Magic down to a dancing walk.

And there was applause as the pony boy helped bring Magic, with Johnny still aboard, back down the track toward the winner's circle.

But that wasn't where they went. They went past the winner's circle, empty except for the table on which the tall, silver trophy—the Dogwood Cup—was sitting.

Johnny's heart was pounding with fear now. He hadn't thought that far ahead. It hadn't occurred to him that he'd be found out at the end of the race. All he had cared about was giving Magic a chance to win.

Then he saw where they were heading—toward the officials' area. There were several men there, and all of them looked terribly serious. Lou was there, and so were the Michaelses.

Johnny's eyes fastened on Jed's face, then went to Caitlin's. What—what was he going to say to them? How was he ever going to find the words to tell them—to explain why he'd done what he'd done?

But then, as Magic stopped, he saw Caitlin smile at him. She stepped toward them. Quickly he slipped from the saddle and faced her.

"Hello, Johnny." She smiled. The smile was just for him. "I wanted to tell you, before anyone else says anything to you, that that was a great ride you gave Magic."

"Th-thank you, uh, Mrs. Michaels. I—uh—"

The photographers and reporters who had been held back were now surging forward, separating him from Magic's owner. The last he saw of her before an official led him to the office, was her giving him a wave of her hand and calling out, "Don't worry, Johnny. Everything will be fine."

16

"I still can't get over how well Johnny rode Magic in that race," Caitlin said, accepting a glass of iced tea from Jed before sitting down.

It was a week after the race, and Caitlin had just finished feeding Laura. She had joined Jed on the terrace for a relaxing few minutes before lunch was served.

"What I can't get over is the guts it took to do what he did. I know the officials were furious, but quite frankly, I understand why he didn't tell anyone. He certainly explained it to my satisfaction."

"I agree." Caitlin nodded. "And I'm glad that Howard was able to straighten out all the legal problems involved after he rode as an unlicensed jockey."

"Yes, me too." Jed took a sip of his tea. "And I think that after the dust settles, after Avil Horton and Red Meyers are dealt with the way they should be, those officials are going to start thinking differently."

"Do you think they'll let him have a license?"

"I hope so. After all, we're backing him."

"I'd love to see him ride Magic again—for real, I mean."

"I can't imagine anyone better for Magic."

"Nor can I."

"I meant exactly what I told him this morning. I want to fire him as a stable boy, but then hire him as our permanent jockey."

"What did he say?"

"What do you think?" Jed asked with a grin. "I think he's in seventh heaven."

"Good!" Caitlin stretched luxuriously and turned her face up to the sun. "And I think that just about describes the way I'm feeling right now."

"Happy, you mean?" Jed took her hand and squeezed it lovingly.

"Very." She turned her head to smile at him.

There was only one thing that kept Caitlin's happiness from being complete—the rift between her and Ginny Brookes was as wide as ever.

But later that summer Jed and Caitlin had two surprise guests—Ginny and Julian.

"Ginny!" Surprised, Caitlin looked at her for a moment, then the two rushed into each other's arms and hugged.

"Oh, Caitlin, you don't know how long I've wanted to make up. Caitlin—" Ginny pulled away from her friend, and Caitlin noticed how flushed her face was. She obviously was excited about something. "Julian and I—we got married."

"Julian?" Caitlin looked at him, and he nodded gently.

Jed stepped forward. "Congratulations," he said and shook Julian's hand.

"Yes! Oh, yes, congratulations," Caitlin said and took his hand. "I'm so happy—for both of you."

"Thank you," Julian replied, then looked into her eyes. "We had to come here, to tell you and to thank you. You see," he explained, "it was your giving me your trust that finally freed me from my old self. Only then could I ask Ginny to be my wife."

"Julian—" Caitlin was overwhelmed.

"Look, I think it's time I thanked you," Jed spoke. "You gave me back my life."

"And what's past is past," Caitlin said. "And now we have only the future to think about." And as Jed put his arm around her waist, she smiled at Ginny and Julian. "A wonderful future for all of us."

FRANCINE PASCAL

In addition to collaborating on the Broadway musical *George M!* and the nonfiction book *The Strange Case of Patty Hearst,* Francine Pascal has written an adult novel, *Save Johanna!,* and four young adult novels, *Hangin' Out with Cici, My First Love and Other Disasters, The Hand-Me-Down Kid,* and *Love and Betrayal & Hold the Mayo!* She is also the creator of the Sweet Valley High and Sweet Valley Twins series. Ms. Pascal has three daughters, Jamie, Susan, and Laurie, and lives in New York City.

DIANA GREGORY

Growing up in Hollywood, Diana Gregory wanted to become an actress. She became an associate TV producer instead. Now a full-time writer, she has written, in addition to other books, three young adult novels, *I'm Boo! That's Who!, There's a Caterpillar in My Lemonade,* and *The Fog Burns Off by Eleven O'clock,* plus several Sweet Dreams novels. Besides writing, her other love is traveling. She has lived in several states, including Virginia, where she stayed on a horse farm for a year. She now calls Seattle home.

We hope you enjoyed reading this book. If you would like to receive further information about titles available in the Bantam series, just write to the address below, with your name and address:

Kim Prior
Bantam Books
61–63 Uxbridge Road
Ealing
London W5 5SA

If you live in Australia or New Zealand and would like more information about the series, please write to:

Sally Porter
Transworld Publishers (Aust.) Pty. Ltd.
15–23 Helles Avenue
Moorebank
N.S.W. 2170
AUSTRALIA

Kiri Martin
Transworld Publishers (N.Z.) Ltd.
Cnr. Moselle and Waipareira Avenues
Henderson
Auckland
NEW ZEALAND

All Bantam Young Adult books are available at your bookshop or newsagent, or can be ordered from the following address:

Corgi/Bantam Books
Cash Sales Department
PO Box 11
Falmouth
Cornwall
TR10 9EN

Please list the title(s) you would like, and send together with a cheque or postal order. You should allow for the cost of the book(s) plus postage and packing charges as follows:

All orders up to a total of £5.00   50p
All orders in excess of £5.00   Free

Please note that payment must be made in pounds sterling; other currencies are unacceptable.

(The above applies to readers in the UK and Republic of Ireland only)

B.F.P.O. customers, please allow for the cost of the book(s) plus the following for postage and packing: 60p for the first book, 25p for the second book and 15p per copy for the next 7 books, thereafter 9p per book.

Overseas customers, please allow £1.25 for postage and packing for the first book, 75p for the second book, and 28p for each subsequent title ordered.

Thank you!